THE CLASSROOM

The Epic Documentary
of a Not-Yet-Epic Kid

THE CLASSROOM

The Epic Documentary
of a Not-Yet-Epic Kid

Directed by Robin Mellom

Filmed by Stephen Gilpin

Disney · Hyperion Books
New York

For all my former students—
I learned so much from you.
—R.M.

For Nemo, Makena, and Talulabel, my middle schoolers.
I don't envy you. Not one little bit.
—S.G.

Text copyright © 2012 by Robin Mellom
Illustrations copyright © 2012 by Stephen Gilpin

Printed in the United States
First Edition
10 9 8 7 6 5 4 3 2 1

G475-5664-5-12105

Library of Congress Cataloging-in-Publication Data

Mellom, Robin.
   The classroom : the epic documentary of a not-yet-epic kid / by Robin Mellom ;
art by Stephen Gilpin.—1st ed.
      p. cm.
   Summary: As a documentary is filmed at their middle school, roles reverse for worrier Trevor and his lifelong best friend Libby, who has always rescued him from embarrassing situations but is now focused on being "cool" and no longer wants to be his "friend friend."
   ISBN 978-1-4231-5063-3 (alk. paper)
   [1. Middle schools—Fiction. 2. Schools—Fiction. 3. Best friends—Fiction. 4. Friendship—Fiction. 5. Self-actualization (Psychology)—Fiction. 6. Documentary films—Production and direction—Fiction.] I. Gilpin, Stephen, ill. II. Title.
   PZ7.M16254Cl 2012
   [Fic]—dc23   2011027768

Reinforced binding

Visit www.disneyhyperionbooks.com

WESTSIDE
MIDDLE SCHOOL

DAY
ONE

>>Production: THE CLASSROOM

Over on Miller Street, behind the brick walls of Westside Middle School, there are desks. There are lockers. There are worksheets, textbooks, pencils, pens, and squeaky hallway floors that are buffed clean every Friday, right around four or so.

And also—since this is a middle school—there are detention slips. The pink ones. An endless supply of them, it seems.

But even more important, behind the walls of Westside Middle School there are people. The kind with weaknesses and strengths; good habits and embarrassing habits; great clothes and really quite terrible clothes.

They are principals, teachers, janitors, counselors, and, of course, students. One of those students is seventh grader Trevor Jones—your normal, everyday, average student.

This documentary set out to show the real story of Trevor, along with his normal, everyday, average classmates.

But what we uncovered was far from average. Mostly it was upper average along with moments of extreme average, but—most important, as you are about to witness—there were several moments of total epicness.

And the following pages will reveal the behind-the-scenes reality of this epic story.

Westside is their middle school.

And these are their stories.

Trevor Jones

7th grader
The end of his
driveway, pacing

7:52 a.m.

Sure, I had it great back in elementary school. Never got in trouble, got straight A's, and had the best baseball card collection around. Ever seen a '73 Johnny Bench? Yep, I kept it wrapped in a sandwich bag. "My lucky card," I called it. But I don't need it.

I'm making lots of changes. Don't even need my lucky pen anymore. Nope. I'm not going to draw and doodle like I did last year. Not even in emergencies. Not even when I'm bored. Everything's different now. This isn't elementary school—no cakewalk. Actually, not even time to line up for water after recess. In fact, no more recess!

[clutches stomach]

Am I worried about the first day of middle school? Nah. I'm planning on doing this all right. No more overthinking. I'm going to be relaxed and not put any thought into it. In fact, I didn't even

5

put any thought into what I wore—just grabbed the first thing I saw.

And I figure as long as I don't get tripped in the hall or pummeled or mangled, it'll go just fine. Right?

[shifts from leg to leg—perhaps cold, perhaps not]

It could happen.

So . . . I gotta bust it to make it to the bus on time.

Nah, I'm not worried about the bus ride either. Unless there are eighth graders around. I've heard stories about them. Eighth graders creep me out. Or if there's a bus driver—the silent kind. Silent bus drivers creep me out almost more than eighth graders. I mean, why NOT talk? Like I said—creepy. And don't even get me started on bus floors being so sticky. Or why there aren't seat belts. Or how a vehicle that old could still function without overheating.

But, okay no . . . no more overthinking. That was last year.

For me, everything's changed. No more baseball cards. No lucky pen. And no doodling. Not even if I'm worried. Which I am NOT.

It'll be fine.

Totally. Fine.

CHAPTER ONE

TREVOR JONES HUFFED IT UP TO THE TOP OF HIS STREET with his lucky doodling pen hidden in the front pocket of his backpack.

He wore brand-new clothes, pre-thought out weeks in advance—he wasn't about to enter the doors of Westside Middle School without being prepared and completely stain-free. Luckily, his mother was a pre-thinker also. Just before he left, she'd gone through the list. Like she had every year.

"I snipped all the price tags off your new clothes," Ms. Jones said.

"Sleeves, too?"

"And I froze your yogurt stick so it will be the perfect temperature by lunchtime."

"Double berry?"

"And I've called all your teachers during pre-planning week to let them know about your issue."

"The excessive worrying?"

"I had to, Trevor. It's in your permanent record," Ms. Jones explained as she straightened his collar. Ms. Jones valued clothes that were crisp as well as food that was the appropriate temperature.

She was also the type of mother who kept her lectures to the point—one, maybe two sentences at the most. "Just do what you did last year. Your teacher wasn't worried *one bit*." Which wasn't true, but Ms. Jones had decided long ago that there were times when exaggeration during a short lecture was necessary if it was for a good cause—namely, helping Trevor with his excessive worrying problem. Which was often.

She rumpled his hair. "So I went ahead and bought a package of Raspberry Zingers, your favorite. If you do well today, it's yours. I know you won't disappoint me."

Trevor's stomach growled. Raspberry Zingers really were his favorite. Ms. Jones rarely allowed Trevor to eat sugar, so she took her motivation tactics seriously, knowing that he would do whatever it took to get access to that sort of sugary snack.

TREVOR JONES

SUBJECTS	Marking Periods			
	1	2	3	4
Math	A	A	A+	A
Science	A+	A+	A	A+
Reading	A	A	A	A
Music	A	A	A	A
Physical Education	A-	A-	A-	A-
History	A	A	A	A
Geography	A	A	A	A
Writing	A	A	A	A
Spelling	A	A	A	A
ABSENCES	O	O	O	O
TARDIES	O	O	O	O

TEACHER
COMMENTS

Trevor's attendance record - WOW!
However, he often doodles in his
notebook and talks about baseball
cards and worries about the
classroom temperature, the
watering schedule for the plants,
and also everything else.
    Is he exposed to excess sugar?
I'm worried about him in Middle
School. _Very_ worried.

But really, he would do whatever it took just to not let
her down. Because Ms. Jones's disappointed face? It could
melt ice.

Mom, let down

Trevor grabbed his backpack, then Ms. Jones happily snipped one more tag and sent him on his way.

In contrast to his new, crisp clothes, his shoes were highly scuffed, marked up, and dirtied—fake wear-'n'-tear. He'd heard it was crucial in middle school to have shoes that looked like you'd just hiked Everest, herded some goats, then stomped some grapes, or maybe the coals of a fire. The dirtier the shoes, the cooler. Because clean shoes? Clearly a computer geek who wore shoes that never saw direct sunlight. Which Trevor didn't think was a problem, but he figured he should do whatever the e-mail told him to do.

He was also told in this e-mail—the one sent the

previous night from his best friend—to watch *Lord of the Rings* countless times so he'd have something to talk about. As if the ridiculous amount of dirt on his shoes wasn't enough?

He glanced down at his shoes to make sure they were adequately scuffed. He scraped them a few more times on the cement, hoping that's all they needed, but he really didn't know.

Truthfully, he wished he could just show up for school without putting any thought into it whatsoever and stop worrying if he had done it all wrong. Why did his permanent record–worthy worry problem always have to follow him around? It seemed his permanent record was a hungry stray cat.

When Trevor reached the bus stop, he saw Libby—friend from down the street, friend from since they were babies, friend who was good at sending reminder e-mails about what to wear and talk about on the first day of middle school.

When they were younger, Libby and Trevor started off as not-by-choice friends, but gradually they became the best of friends. They knew each other so well they could play video games for hours, an activity they'd enjoyed since infancy, and not have to say much of anything.

They'd play for hours, just a couple of indecipherable words, maybe a grunt or a hand gesture here or there—but they rarely needed to talk.

Libby marched up to Trevor as he stood at the bus stop. "We need to talk."

Until today.

"We've been friends for like, forever. Right?" Libby straightened her freshly ironed denim miniskirt. Trevor noticed she was wearing a ribbon in her hair for the first time. And her fingernails were glittery. *Strange.*

"Sure, Lib. We potty trained together. How could I forget?" Trevor squinted his eyes at her, first because he really did not want to recall their potty training past, and second because he was unsure of who or what exactly had replaced his friend.

Libby Gardner was not the type to wear skirts or braid ribbons in her hair or use glitter in place of a perfectly good permanent marker. Her motto: *A good pair of tennis shoes and a sturdy coat are all you need.*

Trevor was convinced she could go on one of those survival shows where she had to make it out of a blizzard in the arctic with just a calculator and dental floss. Whereas Trevor would require a generator and Internet access—not really reality-show worthy.

Libby's only girlish weakness was her Hola! Kitty Cat! pencil box. And wallet. And shoelaces. And sketchpad. But Libby didn't consider this a girly streak as much as simply an act of accumulating objects that might one day become collector's items. No shame in that.

But now, on their first day of seventh grade, she was wearing a skirt. It was ironed. It was clean.

This was newsworthy.

Because when Libby and Trevor were little and playing in the mud, Libby wouldn't just make mud pies, she'd make mud *civilizations* with democratic government structures in place and everything. She felt most comfortable when covered in dirt, creating voting rights for imaginary mud people.

Trevor quickly pinched his own elbow, worried he might actually still be at home in bed having a bizarre dream.

"We're starting middle school now. I think you need to make some changes this year. Like me." She nervously straightened her skirt, looking quite uncomfortable in it.

Trevor nodded, ready to hear what she had to say because even though she was acting highly unusual, he knew he should do whatever she said. It wasn't because she was bossy (Libby preferred the term "brilliant") or because she was right (Libby preferred the term "brilliant") or even because she was brilliant, which she pretty much was.

No, it was because of her attention to detail. Namely, the details she would willingly give every time she stepped in to cover for him.

Like the Great Speaking Disaster of Fourth Grade? The one where Trevor forgot his note cards at home and stood—literally—speechless in front of the entire class? It was Libby who jumped up and explained to the teacher that Trevor was sick and had lost his voice because he had rescued Fiddles, her aging tabby cat, from the rooftop of her house during a freak rainstorm the previous night. Luckily there actually had been a freak rainstorm, and the teacher congratulated Trevor, then gave him an extra week to prepare his speech.

And, of course, there was the Horrifying Mashed-Potato Slipping Incident of Fifth Grade. There Trevor was, splayed out on the cafeteria floor, but Libby didn't miss a beat and made it abundantly clear to everyone nearby that he had slid in order to kill a black widow spider and had saved an unsuspecting student from a venomous arachnid. Yes, she used the word *arachnid*, which was very convincing, and earned Trevor an extra helping of Tater Tots. For a week.

Libby didn't mind inflating the truth, but *only* when it was for the right reason.

Even though she was now standing in front of Trevor with strangely clean and ironed clothes saying they should make some changes, he wasn't worried. When it came to his social life, she had his back.

"We've always hung out together in the past, but I think it's time . . ." Her voice trailed off.

"Time for what?"

She stood up straight, cleared her throat, and said with confidence, "We need to cement ourselves in the social scene."

These were words he did not understand. "Cement what? In *what*?"

"Make friends, Trevor. With other people." Libby had said these words once before. Actually, four times before— on the first day of school since third grade. She'd proclaim they should make other friends—sometimes she'd vary how she said it, maybe emphasizing the word "friends" or "other" or "Trevor," but it always was the same thing.

Then, within hours, he'd get himself in some sort of humiliating situation and Libby wouldn't be able to help it; she'd swoop in for the great cover-up. And everything would go back to normal.

Trevor rocked back on his heels, nodding with complete certainty that this was the same as every other first day of school.

"We're still friends," Libby said in a soft voice. "I just think now we should stop being *friend* friends."

Different. That was different. What was with the use of the double *friend*? Trevor wondered.

Libby could see Trevor was trying to make sense of what she'd just said. His face crinkled in that confused way as he tried to decipher her double use of *friend*. But Libby knew it was going to take a new version of the argument in order to make it sink in. Because *this* time—as much as

16

it made her stomach hurt—she meant it. "You know . . . we'll expand the circle. Or our horizons. Or something." She bounced on her toes for added effect, hoping he wouldn't see she was also clutching her stomach and that he'd realize this was a good idea.

"But—" Trevor tried to interrupt, without success.

"Everything's changed. This is *middle school.*"

She emphasized middle school. This was *definitely* a different type of reasoning. Trevor wondered if she really meant it this time. Did she really expect him to make it through middle school, much less the next few critical minutes, without her protecting him from all embarrassing situations?

"I mean, I can't spend my spare time running around saving you from every embarrassing situation any more."

Apparently so.

Trevor kicked at the dirt. "But mashed potatoes . . . they're so . . . slippery."

"I'm going to do it and you're going to do it. We're going to finally have other friends."

"What do you mean? I already *have* other friends!"

"Really? Who?"

"Ryan," he said.

"He moved to Germany." She shifted her backpack to the other shoulder and crossed her arms.

"Umm, well, Tommy White."

"The first grader you tutored last year?" Now her foot was tapping.

"There's Reese. I'm friends with him."

She threw her arms up in the air. "Trevor, he was our school janitor!"

FOUND IN LIBBY'S HOLA! KITTY CAT! SKETCHPAD, HIDDEN IN HER TRAPPER KEEPER

Trevor Jones. My best friend. And totally in need of a social director.

HOLA! Kitty Cat!

"You shouldn't volunteer to buff floors anymore," she said.

"Come on, Lib. Don't start the big sister thing with me now. I *am* three weeks older than you and, by next year, I'll be almost an inch taller. At least, that's the plan."

Trevor craned his neck to look for the bus; he did not like being late. In fact, he could get anything done as long as he was given a deadline. Homework, chores, making it to the bus with time to spare. He was even born on the exact due date the doctor gave. And Trevor was the type who always—*always*—got to school on time, even if something was growing out of his ear.

bs   Trevor Jones   Bud
"Here on time.
No matter what."

It explained the Perfect Attendance Award.

"I'm glad you have a growth spurt plan," Libby said.

"But you really should focus on becoming friends with a cool guy."

He immediately tried to think of some cool guys. Jimmy Butler . . . no, chewed erasers. Zack Webber . . . no, firestarter. Noah Dawson. . . no, horrible attendance record.

"Look, maybe you could use some advice." Libby laced her fingers together, her project-ready stance. Her *favorite* stance, actually. "Some help? You're pretty close already—your shoes are totally scuffed. Nice."

"I read your e-mail."

"All of it?"

"There were bullet points. And key words in bold. Yes, I read it."

"So then you're not going to rely on your baseball cards for conversation starters, right?"

"I have other things to talk about! Like I'd actually bring my card to school! Jeez!" Trevor smoothly reached down into the side pocket of his backpack and flipped over the '73 Johnny Bench.

"And you didn't bring the Uni-ball pen, did you?"

The Vision Elite Uni-ball roller pen was hands-down the finest doodling pen ever created, in Trevor's opinion. It was also lucky. And luck was something he wished he didn't need anymore. But it wasn't looking that way.

"I wasn't going to use it," Trevor said. "Not *much*. Plus you spent most of sixth grade filling your Hola! Kitty Cat! sketchpad with doodles."

"They were *drawings*. And I threw away that Hola! Kitty Cat! sketchpad." She knew she was stretching the truth. She *would* have thrown it away if it hadn't had such collector's item potential. And if she didn't love drawing in it so much. But telling him she threw it away was for his own good, because he needed to make changes, especially since she hadn't told him all of the bad news yet.

She sighed deeply. The kind of sigh that signified the start of taking on the biggest project of her life. Libby was one who thought "taking on a project" sounded mature and would lead to some sort of emotional growth. She lived for it.

While Trevor thought "taking on a project" sounded like something that should just involve some glue and scissors. Not *him*.

She took a deep breath and planted her hand on her hip—which was what she always did when she was about to tell him something he did not want to hear. "There's one more thing."

Trevor Jones

Scuffing his shoes
on the curb

7:55 a.m.

No, it's fine. This is how it works with us. She tells me to make other friends, I suddenly end up in an embarrassing situation, she bails me out, and *bam!* Back to normal.

We'll probably do this till we're old and cranky and playing video games in a nursing home. So I'm not worried.

Not a lot.

But she'd better change her mind soon. I've heard the middle school bus is pretty much a big, yellow vehicle of doom.

CHAPTER TWO

"**T**HE FALL DANCE."

"The fall *what*? A dance?"

"You know, the Seventh Grade Fall Dance. You ask a girl, hang with friends, dance like crazy, have fun." Libby knocked on his head. "Does any of this ring a bell?"

Trevor didn't want her to know it *was* ringing a bell. It had been ringing his bell for months. But he figured he'd end up carpooling with Libby and wouldn't have to worry about asking someone.

"And you can't go with me this time."

"Not even *carpool*?"

"A *real* date this time, Trev. Middle school is totally different." She bit at her lip nervously. "It's not a carpool thing."

He had to ask a real girl? Someone other than Libby? The dance was only a couple of weeks away, which to him seemed like an unreasonable time frame—it takes longer than two weeks to get up enough guts to ask a girl to a dance. Doesn't that take a lifetime of guts?

But he went ahead and pretended he already had all the guts he needed. "Don't worry about me, Libby," he said as he put his hands on his hips, like a Fall Dance Superhero, then he plopped the icing right on the cake. "Really. It's all under control. Run along. Nothing to see here."

She scrunched up her eyebrows. "I'm serious. Don't joke."

He wasn't joking. He was faking. Faking that he was confident he could handle this. But on the bright side, at least he had a couple of weeks to find someone.

"There's more," she said. "You have to find a date by the end of today."

"What? Did you say *today*? Who makes up these rules?!"

"*Everyone* knows you have to find a date by the end of the first day or else you won't get someone cool. Why else do you think I dressed all nice today? You *have* to find a date. Preferably someone nice. Well-dressed. Great personality. Got it?"

He shrugged, not sure how he was going to go about

the first day of middle school without getting in some sort of horrendously humiliating situation *while simultaneously* finding a date—especially a date with that many requirements. He'd never figure it out. "I'll figure it out."

Libby squinted her eyes, unsure if Trevor remembered that he had a problem with attracting girls who threw punches. "Remember Nancy Polanski?"

How could he forget? Nancy Polanski, who was also starting seventh grade, had thick strong arms due to competitive gymnastics, the uneven bars being her specialty. But she also had a habit of letting boys know she liked them by punching them hard on the arm. If she *really* liked a guy, it was a punch to the stomach. Last year, she punched Trevor so hard in the stomach, he spent the day in the nurse's office icing down his abdominal bruises. And he vowed to stay an arm's length away from her for the rest of forever, plus a week.

"It's your first real dance. It sets a precedent." Libby flinched and added, "All your future dances depend on your date choice today."

"Sounds extreme, Lib. And also dumb. Who is telling you this stuff?"

"Lana. My cousin in Flagstaff. She's been through it. She's a senior in high school so she *knows* what she's talking about. If you land an uncool date this year, the odds of upgrading to a *cool* date next time decrease by something like seventy percent. And then another ten percent every dance after that until . . ." Her voice faded as she looked away.

Trevor poked her on the shoulder. "Until *what?*"

She took a deep breath and then let all the words tumble out. "Until senior prom, when you'll be spending the night reading the latest edition of *Electronic Gaming Monthly* and sucking down Slurpees at the 7-Eleven—by *yourself.*"

Trevor swallowed hard. "Is all that for real?"

"Lana said she's seen it happen. It's sad. That's why you *have* to ask someone cool to the dance. *Today.*" Libby raised an eyebrow and leaned in closer. "In fact, since the only way you'll do anything is if you have a deadline, then here it is: You need to find a date to the dance . . ." Libby pulled out her calculator; she punched in numbers. ". . . in exactly . . ." She looked at her watch. ". . . 434 minutes." Libby liked to convert hours to minutes. She thought it made things sound more dramatic. Trevor thought it made things sound more like a standardized math test problem.

"Libby, no!" He couldn't believe it. She knew him too well—she knew he had a serious deadline disorder.

She put her calculator away and placed her hands

firmly on Trevor's shoulders, as if she were a football coach. "*I'm* going to do it and *you're* going to do it. Before, we've always just hung out together, but we can do this!" She narrowed her eyes, as all good football coaches do. Trevor tried to escape her gaze, but she was locked in. "Everything's changed, Trevor. We're going to cement ourselves . . . we're going to make new friends. And we're going to find dates to the dance by the end of today."

Trevor waved her off. "I'm fine. I'm not the same guy I was last year. There's nothing to worry about."

"If you don't listen to *my* advice, listen to *someone's*, would you?" she said.

"Fine."

"Not your Magic 8 Ball this time."

"I knew that." He made a mental note to hide his Magic 8 Ball. Then he cleared his throat and said in a low voice, "But . . . we're *not* going to be friends?"

"It's not like we're not friends. It's just what I said before . . . we won't be *friend* friends."

Trevor was still double confused, but she seemed satisfied, so he nodded as if he knew *exactly* what she meant. Of course, he didn't. But he still wanted to know if it meant they were going to still sit together on the bus or not. Since first grade he'd *always* sat next to her on the bus ride to school. And in the lunchroom. And field trips. And assemblies. Knowing he always had someone to sit next to just made life easier—he could mark off one thing on his long list of worries. *That wasn't going to get added back to the list, was it?*

"But you're still gonna sit next to me on the bus, right?"

She shook her head.

"How about I sit with you but I don't talk to you?" he offered. "And I won't look at you. Or use your name out loud."

She straightened the shoulder strap on his backpack. "You don't need me to come to the rescue anymore. Just . . . just keep your eyes out for mashed potatoes."

As she walked away, she checked her watch and said under her breath, "Only 431 minutes left. Have a good first day, Trev."

Libby wandered over to a group of students already waiting in line to get on the bus. Trevor stood on the sidewalk by himself wondering how he'd ever make her deadline.

But most importantly, how was he going to get through this without her?

It simply didn't seem possible.

Because other than the Great Speaking Disaster and

Mashed Potato Slipping Incident, he could *never* forget the infamous Bathroom Mix-Up of Sixth Grade. Libby had yanked him back out of the girls' bathroom and silenced all the laughter in the hallway when she wagged her finger and told them Trevor had gone in there because he heard her choking. Libby even added the impressive detail that she was snacking on grape tomatoes and had accidentally swallowed one whole while trying to fix the broken door handle on the third stall. Trevor wasn't quite sure what a broken stall door had to do with choking on a tomato in a bathroom, but everyone nodded and seemed impressed— mostly with Trevor's lifesaving skills—and the principal rewarded him with free lunch. For a week.

Trevor couldn't help but feel he needed his friendship with Libby, if not for all the free stuff. For a week.

And he was sure getting a date on his own without the help of Libby saving him from severe embarrassment was impossible. Even with all the coolest, dirtiest shoes in the world and lack of doodling pen and hidden baseball cards, he wouldn't be able to find the guts to ask a girl.

So he decided he'd just lie low. Not get himself into any situations where he might embarrass himself. Just hang around quietly, be uninteresting, like a houseplant.

People making it through their first day of middle

school without humiliating themselves is super common, he reminded himself. *There's nothing to worry about.*

But that's when the big, yellow vehicle of doom came barreling down the road.

Libby Gardner

7th grader

Just about to board
the bus, dressed in
a new but clearly
uncomfortable denim
skirt

8:02 a.m.

Okay, here's the reason I went with the "we're friends, just not *friend* friends" approach. I'm not really sure what it means, but it sounded sort of official and maybe he'd figure out why I was doing it and be, you know . . . understanding. See, Lana told me that NO guy would ask me to the dance if they found out Trevor might tag along, like he was my little brother or something. What if that's true?

I'm not exactly the type to wear a skirt. I like things that are practical, comfortable, all that. Skirts are horrid—no warmth at all. But if I'm going to get a date—a real one—not like last year where Trevor . . . oh gosh . . . I don't even want to get into it. I mean, I E-MAILED him that it was casual, NO ties. I had to explain to everyone that Trevor's great Nana suddenly died from pulmonary disease—or maybe I said influenza? —and that he'd just come from her funeral so everyone felt sorry for him and people even fetched snacks for him!

So fine. I'll put on a horrid skirt for a day to get a date. I can handle ONE day.

And I mean Trevor does sort of hang around like he's a relative. Which is understandable because he sort of IS, but . . . how am I ever going to get a date to a dance with him always around? I HAD to change us to just "friends." What if he followed me around forever? Like he'd come to my prom? My wedding? The birth of my first brilliant future president daughter? And he'd just hang out in the background playing video games and drawing pictures??

Oh gosh, that sounds so mean, doesn't it? Oh, PLEASE don't edit this all strange and put in creepy music and make me into the mean girl.

That's not the case. But Lana says it's time to cut the cord . . . the video game cord, I guess you'd say. So I've decided to make us just friends, not *friend* friends—the kind who are friends, but . . . not . . . really . . . Oh, I seriously don't know what it means, but it's the only way.

Ditching Trevor on the first day feels so wrong, but my cousin Lana didn't make it sound like I had much choice. And also, she scares me. But I know he'll figure out a way to do this on his own. He may even thank me.

Sometimes we have to make hard choices to get what we want. And yes, that statement explains why I'm wearing ribbons and glitter and a skirt that provides no warmth.

[stares down at her skirt, twirls for a moment, and talks under her breath]

Even though, gosh . . . this denim is fantastic. Impractical, but totally fantastic.

CHAPTER THREE

AS THE BUS APPROACHED, TREVOR NOTICED A KID who lived one street over. Marty, a big, thick eighth grader with a heavy, overstuffed backpack, wearing camouflage pants and clunky shoes—laces untied. And he had a newly shaved head.

Trevor approached him—carefully, catlike—not wanting to startle him. He figured the shaved head must have been a sign of confidence. Or maybe fierceness. Or bad aim. He wasn't quite sure. But Trevor just wanted to find out where the newbie seventh graders should sit on the bus to avoid being pummeled. Plus, since he already *knew* Marty—in Boy Scouts Marty was very handy with sharp tools and had taught Trevor how to whittle his first duck—he figured this would be the easiest way to quickly make a new friend and be done with it. Mission accomplished! (Or soon *would* be.)

"Hey, Marty," Trevor said.

"'Sup, Trevor?" Marty gave a slight nod and stuffed his hands inside the pockets of his camouflage pants, one of the seven pairs he owned because he liked to be prepared for any situation where he might need to hide from predators. Marty was an expert at all things survival, whittling ducks being one of those survival skills. But he also felt he was an expert in surviving middle school now that he was in eighth grade.

And even though Marty didn't talk much—especially early in the morning—he figured he should tell seventh graders everything he'd learned. Namely: stay away from eighth graders.

Since it was now his second year at middle school, Marty was no longer concerned with seating arrangements or which shoes to scuff or whether he'd find the bathroom. His one and only eighth grade concern was whether the pizza at lunch was going to be cheese or sausage. To Marty, meatless pizza was pointless. Which was why he carried a plastic bag of venison jerky strips in his front pocket. Just in case.

"Listen, do you know anything about this bus thing?"

Trevor asked as he shifted from leg to leg. "I mean, where should I sit? It's not assigned seating or anything, right? And also, I shouldn't become such good friends with the bus driver like last year, right? It's uncool to talk to teachers and bus drivers and stuff, right? But what if—"

Marty grunted and cleared his throat, which didn't help all that much because his voice still came out gruff. "Two things: Just chill."

Trevor nodded. "Okay. So be friendly but not *too* friendly? Talkative but not *so* talkative that I annoy the—"

"No. Just *chill*." Marty wiped some barbecue sauce off his sweatshirt. "And just grab any seat you can."

"Great. I'll sit with you," Trevor said with far more volume than he'd intended.

Marty looked around, hoping no one was listening in. "But don't sit near me. I'm an eighth grader." He clamped down on Trevor's shoulder, and said the next words as if they were *monumental*. "Do not ever . . . *ever* look at the eighth graders, much less sit near one."

There went that plan. Trevor figured that since Marty was an eighth grader and he wasn't allowed to sit near him or look at him, developing a friendship would be just too much work.

Plan abandoned.

Trevor thanked Marty and, for a fleeting moment, thought about showing him his '73 Johnny Bench—just for fun—but decided that did not fall in the Just Chill category.

The bus rolled in and pulled to a stop and the line of kids filed on silently. As Trevor climbed on, he saw there were a lot of new kids. Most of them seemed bigger and older, with deeper voices. And the bus was crowded, *very* crowded. Now that all the elementary schools combined at the middle school, there were a lot of faces he didn't recognize. Unknown faces were not Trevor's favorite.

The bus driver stared straight ahead with his hands gripping the steering wheel. He was old with a scowly face, maybe because he'd forgotten his coffee. Or maybe because he hated kids.

"Good morning," Trevor said to the side of his face. No response. *Great. The silent creepy type.*

As Libby walked ahead of him down the aisle, he noticed something he had never seen before. Guys—*older* guys— were looking at her.

Trevor's brain filled with questions: *Is it the skirt? The denim? Does she have a mustard stain they don't want to tell her about?*

And then his brain filled with things he wanted to yell: *Stop looking at her! Don't you know she's gotten to level twenty-seven of Star Invaders? That she knows the names of all the presidents in birth order and alphabetical order and height order? That she's been my best friend since birth? You don't know her!*

Trevor wasn't sure why he was mad about her becoming friends with other people, he just was. None of this seemed fair. What had he done wrong? He started to slump into the empty seat right behind Libby, but before he could sit down, the kid next to him flung his foot on the empty spot to keep Trevor from sitting there.

"Ow!" Trevor jumped up and looked around, in a daze, wondering what he had just sat on. Then it hit him—those weren't just any feet. They dwarfed his in size . . . which meant those were eighth grade feet!

Panic hit Trevor. His heart sped up. His palms went clammy.

He looked up at Libby to see what he should do, but it was pointless. She kept face-forward. No encouraging thumbs-up. Nothing.

It was clear Libby didn't want to be *friend* friends— whatever that meant. And it was starting to look like it meant she wasn't going to help him out for real this time.

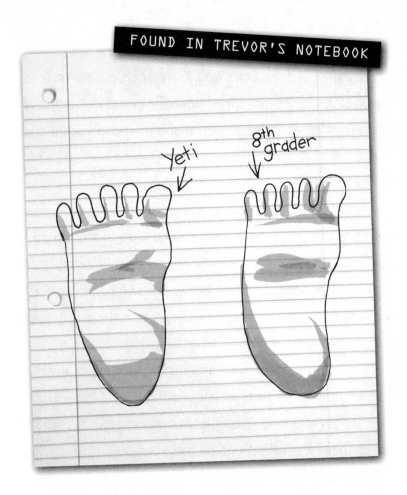

Fortunately, the cranky old bus driver saw exactly what was happening.

"All right, you smart aleck. Move your feet and make room for that kid!" he screamed at his rearview mirror to the eighth grader.

"Oh, no. Oh, no," Trevor mumbled to himself. Marty had told him he wasn't even supposed to *look* at an eighth grader. And now he had attempted to sit on one. Trevor prayed for a sudden natural disaster. A hurricane would've worked, or maybe a werewolf appearance, but no such luck.

"Why should I, Grandpa?" the eighth grader yelled from behind his seat.

The driver hobbled to the back of the bus. He had a gnarled face and smelled like cigarette smoke. He leaned over the seat of the boy and hissed, "'Cuz if you don't, you little vermin, I'm gonna make this the longest bus ride you've ever taken. So long, in fact, you'll need to use the bathroom so bad you'll be begging for it to stop . . . which is when I'll drive down the bumpiest dirt road in town, *and floor it!* So, you wanna go for a long ride or you wanna move your dirty little feet so this nice kid can sit down?"

Creepy, creepy, the driver was still officially creepy. But Trevor appreciated that he was *creative* about it. He was sort of . . . helpful, actually.

The kid mumbled something and moved over with his friend. Trevor slid into the seat behind Libby and felt eyes all around him penetrating his head like lasers.

Trevor leaned up and whispered to the back of Libby's head, "Great! How am I ever going to make a new best friend if I get completely mangled first?"

Libby didn't respond. She was busy chatting with the

girl in the seat next to her. She was on a mission to make other friends and she knew to take advantage of every situation—forced bus seat conversations were always full of friend-making potential.

Wow, Trevor thought. I might actually have to survive this middle school thing on my own. I am doomed.

He slid his hand inside his backpack and touched his lucky '73 Johnny Bench.

And then suddenly . . . no, wait . . . nothing. It wasn't working. No luck.

In fact, he realized he had stumbled into the worst luck a middle schooler on day one could face: he suddenly needed to use the bathroom.

Trevor Jones

Waiting to get
off the bus, dancing
around a little

8:10 a.m.

Yeah, I'm pretty shocked she didn't help me out with that eighth grade foot thing that just happened. I figured she would just stand up and explain I was a foreign exchange student or something. It could've worked. I can fake an accent.

But maybe she was facing the wrong direction and didn't see it happen? That's totally possible.

But, no. Of course she's not REALLY serious about it this time. She can't be—our moms are best friends. We spend every major and minor holiday together. That includes Arbor Day. So her leaving me to fend for myself is practically against the law.

She'll figure that out and things will get back to normal very soon.

But if they don't, even though they WILL, but if they don't . . . my problem is that the only person willing to give me advice is Marty, who

41

eerily smells like beef jerky. Or maybe it isn't beef—what IS it?

But at least he has a backpack stuffed with school supplies, which means he likes to be prepared. And that's a good sign.

Marty Nelson

8th grader

Shaved head, big feet; still sitting on the last seat of the bus, the bouncy one

8:14 a.m.

Let's see, I got the newest edition of *Duck Hunter* magazine, and *Boys' Life*, and *Extreme Hunter*, but I can't find my new copy of *Field & Stream*. . . .

[looks up from his backpack, a confused look]

Oh, you mean am I prepared for middle school? Shoot, yeah. I mean it's not like I have paper or pens or SCHOOL supplies in this backpack, but I'm prepared for any dangerous life situation that comes up. Like, for example, if we're suddenly attacked by a swarm of killer bees? *Boys' Life* magazine here would tell me exactly which page to turn to in that sort of emergency.

Nah, I don't have anything to worry about at middle school—I've already done it. But yeah, I'll give Trevor advice if he needs it. I mean, that seat incident that just went down? Gnarly! Didn't he hear a thing I said? Any advice I give him will be the only advice he'll need. Look at me. I'm close to a spitting image of a success story. I'm in eighth grade. Guys like me are BORN to be eighth graders.

Hey!

[punches the arm of a seventh grader in front of him and snags his backpack from him]

You take my *Field & Stream*?!

CHAPTER FOUR

STEPPING OFF THE BUS, TREVOR FOLLOWED CLOSELY behind Libby, and they oozed into a sea of faces they didn't know. That is, until one girl from elementary school bounced up to them. Cindy Applegate. She was the Official School Gossip last year and was clearly reprising her role again—with official bounce and everything.

Cindy Applegate was very short, not much taller than her locker handle, but that extreme bounce to her step made up for it, somehow making her seem bigger. And Cindy Applegate *always* wanted to seem bigger. She hoped to someday be at least eye level with the books on the top shelf of her locker. But for now, she'd have to rely on bounce.

Trevor figured she was destined to one day become the host of *Fashion Alert* or *Celebrities Gone Bad* on the Entertainment Channel. Or a school secretary.

Her dream, actually, was to become school class president, because that way when she spoke she could stand on a step stool to reach the microphone, making her a good foot and a half taller. Which would be—in her words—wicked awesome.

Cindy bounced up to Libby and Trevor. "Oh-ma-god! Guess what!"

Libby and Trevor nodded at her but neither one of them guessed what. So she continued without even taking a breath. "We're all in the same homeroom! Isn't that just the awesomest thing? And it's with Mr. Everett. I hear he's the best. A little strange, though. Big ears. Drinks tea. Let's all sit together, 'kay?"

Cindy always seemed to know everything about everything, plus the details. As far as gossiping went, she was a pro.

Libby and Cindy were political friends, meaning they would smile at each other but never show teeth. Polite, but not pleasant. They had both run for student council president every year since fourth grade, and if there had been a student council in preschool they would've run then too.

SOCIAL SKILLS TRAINING!

Is Your Friend an Official School Gossip?

Check for warning signs:

Judgmental eyebrows

Large eyes for sneaky glancing

A big mouth

Highly used vocal cords

How Can You Protect Yourself from a Gossip?

Walk away.

If that doesn't work, offer gum, walk away.

PAMPHLET FOUND OUTSIDE OF COUNSELOR'S OFFICE

It seemed the student body could never make up its mind, electing Cindy as president in fourth grade, Libby in fifth, and back to Cindy again in sixth. Libby figured since there was a pattern forming, it should be *her* year to win seventh grade student council president.

But Cindy didn't believe in patterns—only in the

wicked awesomeness of step stools that made you a foot and a half taller. Considering that Cindy hadn't grown six to twelve inches over the summer as hoped (she grew 0.3 cm, but some say it was just the flip-flops), she knew winning class president would give her the *bigness* she was craving. And that meant she would have to defeat Libby. But with a polite smile, of course.

Trevor shrugged at Cindy, and Libby didn't say a word, just smirked at her and headed down the hall by herself, not saying bye, not giving Trevor directions to their homeroom class, not even giving him a chance to tell her he had to use the bathroom. Instead, she left him standing there next to Cindy. Alone. He'd only set foot in this school once, during Open House, but that was held in the gym, so he had no idea how to navigate the halls. What was he supposed to do? Read the *map*?

Trevor couldn't believe Libby would leave him by himself with a highly trained gossip. He was *certain* to spill some piece of vital information that Cindy could easily use against him. Why wasn't Libby protecting him from certain impending doom?

"So?" Cindy smacked her gum three times, then continued. "What's the story with Libby? She's acting different. Strange. Don't you think?"

Of course that's what I think, Trevor wanted to say, and actually came very close to spilling all the details about Libby not wanting to be *friend* friends anymore and him not knowing what it meant. But fortunately he stopped himself before letting it spill out.

"Hold on," he said, then quickly ran down the hall and caught up to Libby. She stopped and faced him with her right eyebrow raised exceptionally high as if to say, *See you later, Trevor.*

Trevor and Libby had been close friends for a *very* long time—that meant eyebrow reading came with the territory.

Can't we walk to class together? he eyebrowed back.

She arched hers even higher and added a forehead crinkle. *No.*

Libby turned and walked away without another eyebrow word. And suddenly Cindy appeared next to him, smacking her gum loudly. "Seriously. What's the deal? Why aren't you walking with her? I thought you guys were Siamese twins or something."

He knew this was fuel for her gossip machine, so he decided to change the subject. Distract her. Quick! Which explains why he leaned over and told Cindy about his "problem."

"Oh-ma-god, Trevor. Didn't anyone tell you that going to

the bathroom and making it to class on time is impossible?" Her voice boomed. People started looking at them.

"Don't talk so loud." Trevor lowered his voice, hoping she'd do the same. "Don't we get some extra time to take care of, you know, 'business'?"

Fortunately, she lowered her voice and switched over to lecture mode, almost instructional, actually. "No. Here's the thing. It's a well-known fact that the late bells are triggered by a sensor that goes off whenever people are in the bathroom hurrying to make it to class on time. And if you're a seventh grader trying to make it to class on time . . . well . . . you don't go."

"But—"

"Seventh graders *hold it*. Everyone knows that." She rolled her eyes and popped a piece of oversized pink gum all over her mouth. She scraped it off and tossed it in the trash. "Bye, Trevor. See ya in homeroom."

Trevor did a little dance that may have been taken in one of two ways: 1. He really had to go to the bathroom and there was no chance of "holding it." 2. He was happy to have Cindy in his homeroom.

He wished number two were true.

Cindy glanced back, taking note of that dance. Because she knew *exactly* what it meant.

Cindy Applegate

7th grader/official gossip

In the hallway, right next to Mr. Everett's class, chewing gum

8:29 a.m.

Okay, so Hubba Bubba Strawberry Watermelon is hands down the best for flavor and long-lasting-ness, but the Island Punch is just wrong and mean. Don't try it.

But you know that Trevor guy? He's cute. Sometimes. I think. I'm not sure. But he'll probably ask me to the dance. Did you see how he kept asking me questions? And all that DANCING? It was like a connection. Interest, they call it. But what was up with that Perfect Attendance Award last year? Kinda weirded me out. His shoes are cool.

Okay, and also? This girl Samantha told me—or maybe it was an Internet chat room that told me—that Libby and Trevor got into some wicked fight this morning and they aren't friends anymore. Just like every other first day of school. But I get the feeling it might actually be real this time.

But, okay, the Hubba Bubba Sweet & Sassy Cherry

51

is pretty good and if I was stuck on an island and there wasn't any gum or food around or even any salad with fat-free dressing, I'd chew it, but, you know . . . it's no Strawberry Watermelon.

No, please, PLEASE don't get me started on bubble tape gum.

Gum is not tape. For reals.

CHAPTER FIVE

TREVOR HUSTLED UP AND DOWN THE HALLS LOOKING for the boys' bathroom without any success. He checked door numbers, looked for signs, jiggled knobs. No luck. Would he *ever* find it?

Kids were laughing and pushing and shoving. He dodged groups of girls and guys as they huddled together, walking in tightly glued pods—totally impenetrable. And they were definitely not paying attention to the fact that they should be on the right side of the hall. There was an *extreme* lack of order.

As he ducked and darted from left to right to keep from getting plowed over, Trevor realized their sense of order and direction was being ignored because most everyone was staring down at their schedule card. But some walked tall with empty hands—they knew exactly where they were going. Eighth graders, he figured.

It hit him that he might seriously get lost. Minutes were ticking by, so Trevor settled for his final and most desperate option . . . read the school map.

"No!" he said to himself. "*Too* desperate."

Instead he went for the final, but slightly less desperate option: ask someone.

The people in the halls began to disperse, quickly heading off to homeroom. Trevor *had* to find someone willing to stop and give him directions.

And there he was—his final less desperate option: Corey Long. An eighth grader. And well-known jerk. He was slouched next to a locker, reeking of coolness. Trevor watched as Corey reached up and checked his hair to make sure it was hanging long over his eyes, but not directly *in* his eyes—a fine distinction. Corey Long looked totally relaxed with his surroundings. Like he controlled the weather.

Corey had gone to their elementary school, but Trevor had never spoken directly *to* him. Mostly because he was a year older, but also because he had a reputation of being the highest level of jerk imaginable. This title being earned due to the fact that he would torment/harass/regularly pummel guys—always the smaller ones. But whenever a girl or a teacher came around, he suddenly became Mr. Perfect/Helpful/Do-No-Wrong.

Trevor had heard Corey one time poured some Mountain Dew on the hallway floor and this kid slipped on it. The guys stood around laughing as they watched the kid splayed out on the floor, but when a teacher came around the corner, Corey pretended the liquid had come from Georgie Johnson's science project. He cleaned it up as if he'd saved the lives of unsuspecting students and even helped the kid up off the floor. So Corey got some certificate for bravery, and the girls and the teachers had no idea he was simply a jerk who had mastered the fake innocent smirk-o-evil. Trevor figured if there had been a sporting event in the Olympics for Extreme Jerkiness, Corey would've brought home the gold, plus some sports clothing endorsements.

Corey watched as Trevor approached him, unsure why Trevor was coming over to talk to him, but he looked like he had a question—probably about the bathroom, because Trevor was doing some strange leg movements. Corey adjusted his hair strands, making sure they looked cool, even though it didn't take much effort. Corey felt he had simply been born cool. Nothing snobbish about it; he just thought some people were born with high foreheads or long toes or good rhythm, but Corey was born cool. Not much else to it, he felt.

Even still, no matter the differing opinions, every girl had a crush on him.

Every teacher happily gave him hall passes and the benefit of the doubt.

And every smallish guy feared him.

So Trevor—being sort of diminutive—couldn't believe he was about to ask Corey for directions to the bathroom. But desperate was desperate, and he had run out of options.

"Hey, man." Trevor figured adding "man" to his vocabulary would show he was a newer, cooler Trevor. Not Perfect Attendance Trevor. Or Baseball Card Trevor. Or Doodler Trevor. "Where are the bathrooms around here?"

Corey smiled. "Just take your first left and then your second right. No, *third* right. Yeah, that's it. Good luck, dude."

Trevor was relieved. Corey had smiled at him. A real smile. It didn't even resemble a smirk-o-evil. Perhaps his Olympic gold medal for jerkiness had been stripped due to him becoming sort of *human*, Trevor thought.

So he followed Corey's directions exactly. It was a good thing Corey didn't have him make the second right— the teachers' lounge. So Trevor took the third right. As he walked up to the stall, he noticed another student had walked in, too. Which was fine, only he had a beard.

Huh. That's strange. Puberty hit him hard, Trevor thought.

Until he realized he wasn't a student . . . but a *teacher*. Corey Long had sent him right into the teachers' bathroom!

Trevor zipped up quickly and sprinted back outside into the hallway. And that's when his foot collided with a much bigger, yeti-like foot.

An eighth grade foot.

Splat.

Trevor landed on the floor. And the entire hallway full of people started laughing hysterically. He looked around and saw Corey laughing so hard he was howling, right along with the crowd he had assembled to witness the moment of Trevor's official public humiliation.

And where was Libby? How could she resist a situation that needed to be fixed? Why wasn't she flying in like a caped Friend-Since-Birth Superhero and helping him?

So there Trevor was, splattered in the middle of the hallway—friendless, no one to defend him—and he didn't say a thing.

Just then, Cindy Applegate rounded the corner and bounced up to the gathered crowd. But her mouth dropped

Yard Sale!
All items of public humiliation
on sale: 2 for 1.

when she saw Trevor splayed out on the floor, flanked by laughing goons. Trevor felt relieved that *someone* was going to be on his side, even if it was Cindy.

But like always, Corey quickly gained control of the situation. "Cindy, you're looking good today. That backpack looks heavy. Need some help?"

She batted her eyes and blushed. "Sure, Corey."

"Spaz, don't be rude." He smacked one of his goons on the back of the head. "Carry her backpack, dude."

Spaz, whose twitchy eyes and spiky hair matched his given name, quickly snatched her backpack and hung his head as he escorted her down the hall.

She looked back and gave a dinky wave. "Aw, thanks Corey!" She had now completely forgotten the fact that Trevor was still on the floor in yard sale position.

When she was gone, Corey turned back and leaned over Trevor. "You should've used your map, newbie." Then he adjusted a strand of hair over his eye and strutted back down the hall, as if on his way to stand at the podium and receive his next Olympic gold medal.

It was then that Trevor got mad. Not at Corey, but at Libby. He couldn't help but think this was her fault. Because Libby knew that Trevor and embarrassing situations were like magnets. If she hadn't left him alone, he wouldn't have had to ask Corey for directions. He considered marching right up to her (after he'd picked himself up off the dirty floor, of course) and telling her off. Maybe even raise his voice.

But then Trevor dropped his head even lower because he remembered that Libby knew his weakness (other than making deadlines): his mother. Libby talked to his mom on the phone a lot, and she told her everything, so being confrontational to Libby was never allowed. Trevor's mother often gave two-sentence lectures on respecting girls; he'd have to eat dry cereal for weeks if he hurt her feelings. No Zingers, that was for sure.

He covered his face with his hands and said to himself, "I am completely doomed."

After a few moments of self-pity, Trevor scraped himself off the floor and scuffled down the hall. But just as he got to the door of his homeroom class, the late bell rang.

Cindy Applegate was right. Bathroom breaks and late bells are like seventh and eighth graders . . . they do not mix.

Corey Long

8th grader/official
reeker of coolness

Leaning against
a locker, double-
checking hair
strand placement

8:35 a.m.

No, I don't feel bad about it. It's a tradition, dude. It happened to me last year. Except they gave me directions to the eighth grade girls' bathroom, but instead of running out, I chatted the girls up and they actually thought I was cool. It was no tragedy for me, but that doesn't mean I don't get to pass the tradition along.

Actually, I almost wasn't going to do it because I couldn't find anyone to take the bait, but then the dude walked up to me and tossed it in my lap. "Where's the bathroom?" Was this guy for real? NO ONE asks that question on the first day of school. It's all over the Internet chat rooms. The guy needs to get some good advice.

So I owed it to my ancestors to continue the prank. I'm doing my part. It's the circle of life thing. Like that lion movie.

I'm the dad lion. No, he dies. I'm that Scar

guy. No, no . . . I'm that bird. Everyone likes that bird. The bird's funny.

[straightens his collar; exudes advanced levels of confidence]

Yeah. I'm the bird.

CHAPTER SIX

HOMEROOM. TREVOR RUSHED INTO THE CLASS, breathless and worried he would be marked tardy. But he saw only the back of the teacher who was busy untangling a wall map and not paying attention to latecomers. Relieved, Trevor looked around and noticed everyone else was already seated and busy filling out a worksheet. He scanned the room for clues as to where to sit. Was it assigned? Open seating? Were there crisp name tags taped neatly to the corners of the desks? A hostess wearing all black who said, "Right this way, sir"?

No.

There was only a diagram drawn on the board.

And Trevor decided he needed to know double advanced mega calculus to understand it.

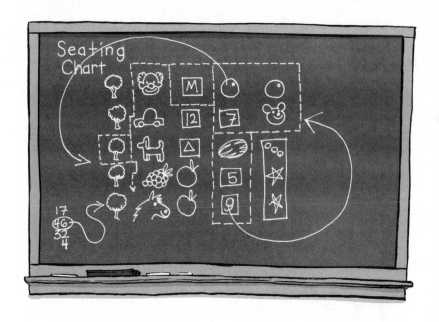

"Need help?"

Trevor looked next to him. It was the teacher, Mr. Everett. Cindy Applegate was right: big ears, cup of tea.

"Uhh . . ." Trevor wasn't sure if it was cooler to take help or to *decline* help.

Mr. Everett, wearing a silk shirt covered in swaying palm trees, took a sip of his steaming hot tea from a mug that said PAUSE FOR A MOMENT OF SCIENCE. He would be both Trevor's homeroom teacher and science teacher. An extremely intelligent man, he had three master's degrees, which he kept stuffed in a desk drawer. Mr. Everett had studied many teaching methods but finally came to the realization that the best way to motivate students was through Skittles. He always had a large supply proudly displayed on his desk.

He popped two green Skittles in his mouth, then said, "You're Trevor, right?"

"Yes." Trevor was excited he knew the correct answer to the first question he was asked in middle school. It was a good start. With the teachers, at least.

"Pretty simple stuff," Mr. Everett explained. "Trevor starts with T as does tangerine, so follow the orange across the diagram to the number six since that's how many letters are in your name and that means your seat is in the T-six zone, which is . . ." Mr. Everett looked around the room, glancing at the few remaining open desks. "Huh, where *did* I put that zone? Oh, forget it; just have a seat next to Molly."

Mr. Everett handed Trevor a worksheet titled "Get to Know Me!" with questions about favorite colors and favorite books and whether he needed a special seating assignment due to vision problems or bad attitude problems.

Trevor slid into a seat in the unknown zone and looked at the girl next to him, Molly. She wore a torn denim jacket and skirt, faded rainbow-colored tights ripped at the knees, and heavy scuffed black boots, and her dark hair had chunky blue streaks.

Uh . . . Trevor thought. Because he didn't really know what to think.

He looked around the room and saw Libby sitting straight and tall in the first row. To her left was Cindy Applegate. He hoped Cindy hadn't already heard the gossip of *how* he ended up splayed out on the hallway floor. Was she *that* good?

Trevor swallowed hard and gently placed his backpack on the floor, trying not to be noticed.

"Is that a *baseball* card?"

Ripped but colorful Molly was now glaring at him as she pointed to the open front pocket of his backpack.

"That? No . . . that's some trash I found. . . ." Trevor realized how gross that sounded. "Um . . . I don't mean trash I found, like I run around picking up trash and storing it in my backpack . . . ha! . . . no, no I don't do that . . ."

FOUND IN TREVOR'S NOTEBOOK

Where this conversation is going.

Molly leaned in closer. "It's a '73 Johnny Bench."

As Trevor pulled the card out of his backpack, he looked over at Molly and noticed a slight smile forming on her face, and he also noticed the heavy blue eyeliner on her ocean-colored eyes. More Atlantic than Pacific, but still . . . quite blue. He snapped out of his eyeball staring trance and finally said in a low voice, "Yeah. How'd you know?"

"The front of the card," she said plainly. "It says '73 Johnny Bench."

"This is true." Trevor flipped the card around in his now sweaty hand, trying to figure out what to say next to keep this conversation going. But he didn't have to. Molly kept talking without needing anyone to ask her a question.

"I collect stuff. Old stuff. Any stuff. Lots of stuff." She picked at her pencil eraser. "And then I fill my room with all the things I collect so that no one else can even get the door open."

Trevor's room didn't have a single item out of place. Opening the door was never a problem for him. So he couldn't quite understand why she might find that appealing. But all he could think about was the fact that he'd met someone—a girl, in fact—who collected rare baseball cards. And had Atlantic Ocean blue eyes.

"I'm Trevor," he said.

"Molly." She tugged at her rainbow tights, accidentally ripping them a little more. But this didn't concern her; she was far more concerned with finding out if Trevor was talking to her because he wanted to become friends or something strange like that.

Molly had just moved to Westside Middle School. The previous year she had attended Jefferson Middle School. Also Lincoln Middle School. Also Washington Middle School. She hadn't made any friends—at least she didn't remember making any—which made her happy because she never *intended* on making any. Her plan last year, as it was for *this* year, was to not make any friends whatsoever. Moving so much, friends never stuck around. But she figured *stuff* would hang on forever.

While the class started working on their "Get to Know Me!" worksheets, Trevor leaned over and placed the baseball card on Molly's desk. "Want to look at it?" he whispered.

Her brightly lined eyes brightened even more. "Really? Let's swap for a day." Molly reached into her army green backpack, which was very ripped but held together with safety pins, pulled out a teeny-tiny Magic 8 Ball key chain, and placed it on his desk.

Trevor often relied on the guidance of a Magic 8 Ball,

but he knew Libby would be unimpressed if she knew he was carrying one around at school. He stuffed it deep in his backpack. "Thanks."

Molly was too busy reading all the stats on the back of the card to respond. Sign of a true baseball card fan, Trevor thought.

He took a deep breath and looked over at Libby to make sure she wasn't witnessing this. Luckily she was already busy with her "Get to Know Me!" worksheet.

But it was then that he noticed Nancy Polanski, three rows over, glaring at him. She clenched her fist, then motioned to a poster on the wall.

Trevor swallowed hard, because he did not want to experience a Nancy-fist-to-the-stomach ever again. And also because the poster was a reminder of the deadline Libby had given him. He really didn't want to think about having to use words—good ones, too—to ask a girl to the dance by the end of the day.

"You have to ask a girl by the end of the day," Molly explained as if she could read his worried thoughts. She motioned to Libby and Cindy. "Why else would they look so cute and clean?" Molly shrugged as she looked down at her ripped tights and clunky boots.

Trevor wasn't quite sure what to say. And he definitely did not want to make eye contact with Nancy Polanski. So he simply turned back to his desk and got busy on his worksheet. *Eyes down, eyes down! Don't look up!* he thought.

Molly noticed that Trevor kept his eyes on his paper and wasn't giving her any eye contact, the sign of someone *definitely* not wanting to be friends. Which instantly made her feel comfortable. So she chatted on and on to the side of his face about the dance and baseball and her clunky boots.

Of course, Trevor immediately worried he was going to get in trouble for talking in class, but fortunately Mr. Everett was back to struggling with his wall map. Trevor, happy that he was having such a successful conversation with a girl without having to actually *look* at her, noticed out of his peripheral vision that she seemed to end her sentences with nice shoulder shrugs. And he realized that suddenly—out of nowhere, and for reasons he couldn't explain—the thought of asking a girl to the dance didn't make him want to squirt hot sauce into *anything*, much less his eyeballs.

Trevor Jones

Homeroom, pretending
to sharpen his
pencil

8:40 a.m.

Okay, Libby's NOT going to believe this. I'm going
to blow her deadline away. I am definitely going
to have a date to that dance by the end of the day.

I mean I don't want to get ahead of myself here
or anything, but didn't Molly seem to be made of
some sort of perfection? Was I the only one who
noticed that? It's like she's made of rainbows and
cake . . . after they get ripped up and smooshed
and torn . . . but still . . . I'm sensing some
sort of perfection there. It seems like this day
is really turning around. Is it hot in here? And
I was totally cool about it all. Not hyper or
strange or anything. She even smiled. I'm almost
sure of it.

Yes, I will have a date to the dance by the end
of the day.

Aw, dang. I just stated a deadline out loud.
Now I have to do it.

But all I have to do is maintain THIS level of

coolness for the rest of the day, and Molly will say yes.

Or . . . no. I guess she could say no.

But, hey. At the very least we'll exchange our stuff back at the end of the day. And that will be awesome.

Oh, the part about making another friend? It's under control. I'm on a roll already. I mean, how hard could it be? You just lend someone a pencil and—*bam!*—you're friends. No problem.

Molly
(last name not stated)

Mysterious new
student

Homeroom, sneaking
thumbtacks off the
bulletin board

8:42 a.m.

Yeah, I know it's only twenty-five minutes into the first day, but this place is a drag. Assigned seating? A teacher who drinks hot tea? And that Trevor guy? He obviously doesn't like me, thankfully. At least he gave me a baseball card.

I guess the only good thing about this place is the stuff.

[opens backpack and peers inside]

So far I've traded for a Yoda bobblehead, a Popeye Pez dispenser, a troll doll, and that '73 Johnny Bench, which actually is a pretty good card. But I'm hoping someone here at this drag of a school will at least have some good vintage Hola! Kitty Cat! supplies. I'd like to round out my collection.

I switch schools a lot. My dad says I'm "attention deficit."

I call it "bored." But I'm convinced that vintage Hola! Kitty Cat! can totally cure that.

CHAPTER SEVEN

"**T**URN YOUR WORKSHEETS IN," MR. EVERETT announced.

Trevor felt all the blood rush to his head. He had drawn on the *back* of his worksheet, but hadn't actually done the assignment. Very unlike him.

He covered his paper with his hands and decided he would finish it between classes and turn it in late. Not ideal, but Trevor figured Mr. Everett was surely a reasonable teacher, just as his teachers last year had been.

"Students, listen up." Mr. Everett carefully placed his hot tea on a coaster and cleared his throat. "This is your first year of middle school and, as you've probably heard, seventh grade is *very* different. We're strict."

Trevor looked around and saw most of the other kids

nodding, as if they all already knew everything about how middle school works. How did they know all this already?

Trevor knew nothing. He'd figured Libby would always tell him anything he needed to know. He had just assumed "anything he needed to know" would be about school supplies and dress codes and how to defeat the imperial wizard on level twenty-one of Star Invaders (not easy). He didn't think he'd have to understand things like "cementing himself in the social scene." Cement was so permanent.

Last year, because they were sixth graders, Trevor and Libby had been pretty much untouchable. The younger kids looked up to them and, most important, sixth graders always got the best seats on the bus.

But now *they* were the younger kids. All those years climbing to the top spot for a smidgen of respect, and now they had to start all over again. Bad bus seats. Bathrooms that were impossible to find. And pummeling by the eighth graders. But Trevor had heard stories about the grumpy vice principal at Westside. It's a good thing the vice principal is strict, Trevor thought. He'll enforce rules about pummeling. I'll be fine.

Mr. Everett popped a couple of red Skittles in his mouth. "And we have a *new* vice principal this year. A very nice guy—you're lucky."

Never mind.

"His name is Mr. Decker, and he plans on making some changes around here. For starters, he wants the seventh and eighth graders to spend more time together. He figures if you're friends, all the pummeling will end." Mr. Everett shrugged. "Could work. I don't know. We'll find out soon enough." He turned and pointed to the poster on the wall. "Mr. Decker has made the Fall Dance a seventh *and* eighth grade dance. You'll all get to hang out *together*."

Trevor flopped his head on his desk.

Get it over with. Pummel me now.

Daily Planner

Home room to do:
- Take roll
- Break the news about Decker

Notes:
Trevor Jones—lots of head flopping, concerned he may develop small concussion by end of the day. Keep on eye on this one.

FOUND IN MR. EVERETT'S DAILY PLANNER

The intercom crackled. "Good morning, responsible and soon-to-be-healthy students. I am Mr. Decker, your new vice principal."

Trevor looked up and noticed Molly was the only one who had her head buried in her arms with hands covering her ears. He figured she was probably sneaking glances at his baseball card. *Some sort of perfection*, he thought.

"There are a couple of announcements. First, the double cheese pizza for lunch has been replaced with artichoke loaf. Cheese is not good for increasing your attention span; vegetables are. You're welcome. And second, a reminder that no students are allowed in the teachers' bathroom."

Trevor's face turned salsa red. Twenty-five minutes into the first day and he had already caused the vice principal to make an announcement about him? Trevor peered around and saw Cindy lean over to Libby and whisper something. *Oh, no. Was she telling her about my humiliating hallway yard sale?* Luckily, he noticed Molly wasn't paying attention to any of this and her ears were still covered.

"Now, don't forget that the Fall Dance will be seventh *and* eighth graders, so get ready to make some new friends. Have a great first day, Westside!"

Vice Principal Decker was in charge of school discipline in addition to overseeing student council elections, sporting events, dances, assemblies, and any other time the students gathered in proximity to one another. But he also put it upon himself to take on the task of improving school morale through healthy eating habits. Kids full of vegetables were kinder to each other, was Decker's line of thinking. He had started this program at many schools in the past, but would inevitably end up transferred. He didn't mind, though, because he could reach *so many* more students that way. And he had high healthy-eating hopes for Westside.

VICE PRINCIPAL DECKER'S DESK

INSPIRATION IS INSPIRING

VICE PRINCIPAL DECKER

I ♥ JOB TRANSFERS

Trevor flopped his head on his desk again. Vegetables for lunch? Make friends with eighth graders?

He looked over at Libby hoping she'd at least eyebrow something encouraging. But she was helping another girl read a school map. Libby was always doing stuff like that—helping people out, even if they didn't ask for it. Which Trevor thought was good and bad.

Bad because one time she forced him to actually *join* a baseball team instead of just looking at cards. But good because Trevor moved up from seventh-string pitcher to sixth-string pitcher in just three months. He went back to seventh-string pitcher right after Bruce Parker's broken arm healed, but still . . . he had to admit . . . Libby always gave good advice. So deep down, he had to admit that her idea of making new friends might . . . possibly . . . be a good idea.

And that's when he heard the pencil drop.

The blond girl sitting in front of Molly didn't realize her pencil had fallen to the floor. Now, Trevor knew *lending* someone a pencil was an easy way to make a friend (he'd paid attention in fourth grade social skills class), so even though this pencil scenario wasn't ideal, at least he could use it to talk to the guy sitting in front of him.

Trevor stuck his foot out and used his heel to pull

the pencil in so he could pick it up. Then he tapped the shoulder of the guy in front of him. "Hey, could you hand this pencil back to that girl?"

But the guy coiled back, looking rather horrified, not friendly at all. "Wh—what?"

Trevor pointed over to the blond girl. "Her. Hand this to that girl!"

The guy shook his head and threw his hands up. "Dude, that girl is a *dude*. That's Jake Jacobs."

Trevor felt the blood rush to his face. Sure enough, the "girl" turned around and . . . yep . . . dude.

Trevor glanced at what Jake Jacobs was wearing: baggy jeans with Vans skater shoes and a very worn Tony Hawk skater T-shirt. *Oh, man. Why didn't I look for clues?* Trevor lectured himself.

In elementary school when someone called a guy a girl, it would get some laughs. But mistaking a dude for a girl in middle school was some sort of felony. A lot of people sort of wore their hair the *same*. Stringy, moppy, long.

Jake Jacobs leaned across Trevor's desk and snatched his pencil back while getting a glimpse of Trevor's paper. "Go back to drawing pictures, kid." And everyone around them laughed—everyone but Molly. She still had her head buried in her arms.

At the end of homeroom, Libby walked by Trevor, dropped a note on his desk, and casually walked out the door.

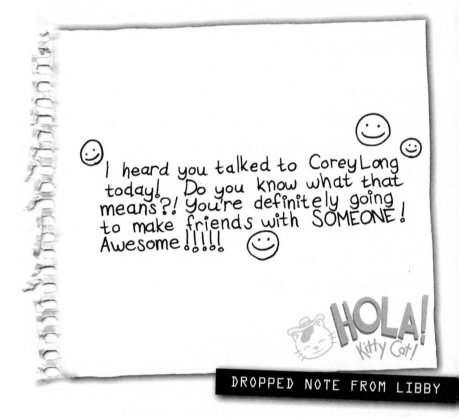

I heard you talked to Corey Long today! Do you know what that means?! You're definitely going to make friends with SOMEONE! Awesome!!!!! ☺

HOLA! Kitty Cat!

DROPPED NOTE FROM LIBBY

Libby happily strolled down the hall to her locker. Though she was anxious to find new friends and a date to the dance for herself, she was glad that Trevor seemed to be taking her advice. And with Corey Long!

Libby knew Corey from a couple of years back—co-ed

82

swim team. Corey was the only boy on the team, but he seemed to enjoy it very much because he was always supportive of his team members.

Whenever Libby would swim, he'd yell out to her, "Swim, Nicole, swim! You can do it!" She appreciated his cheering, but felt too embarrassed to tell him he was calling her by the wrong name. So she spent as much time as possible underwater so she wouldn't have to hear it. But it slowed her time down and she was eventually bumped back to beginner swim team, which was why she quit. But at least she had increased her lung capacity; she could stay underwater for eighty-three seconds. Not too shabby.

So even though Corey didn't know her actual name, he was still a nice guy, and she was excited that there was a rumor he was being nice to Trevor. A very good sign, she thought.

Before Trevor left homeroom he crumpled up Libby's note and stuffed it in his backpack. She'd heard Corey just *talked* to him? Like he was some kind of nice guy or something? Trevor figured Cindy's gossip machine would get cranked up; he just didn't know it would happen this quick. And that she wouldn't get her facts straight. *At all.*

"Try these."

Trevor looked up. Mr. Everett must have noticed he was

upset because he was standing at his desk offering him a handful of red Skittles. "These will calm you right down." He patted Trevor on the shoulder and returned to his desk to finish his now not-so-hot tea.

Trevor munched on the Skittles while he mumbled to himself. "This is a nightmare. She thinks Corey was being cool to me? The guy's evil! These Skittles are good. But if I don't start making other friends and find a date, I know exactly what she'll do—she'll call my mother. Just like she did that time she caught me talking to that turtle."

Trevor stopped mumbling to himself when he looked up to see Molly, still sitting at her desk, but now glaring at him, her mouth hanging open.

"You talk to *turtles*?" Her tone was of the grossed-out type.

"Yes. No! One time. It was a rainy day. Lots of flooding. The turtle was scared."

She gave him a confused look.

"Help turtle. Need. He was." Unfortunately, when Trevor was nervous, he reverted to Yoda-speak. Very embarrassing.

Molly quickly gathered her stuff and said, "Uh, thanks for giving me that baseball card," as she hurried out of the room.

Trevor covered his face with his hands. When would

he ever use the right words at the right time? Was making friends really going to be this hard? But more importantly, did Molly say he *gave* her the baseball card?

He pulled out the miniature teeny-tiny Magic 8 Ball Molly had given him and whispered to it, "Is Molly going to give me my baseball card back?" But the answer on the tiny screen was too small to read. And that's when it became clear to him: he needed a bigger ball.

Trevor Jones

Face planted
against the
front of his
locker

8:50 a.m.

I need help. Some advice or something. Libby thinks Corey Long was being nice to me and this will somehow lead to popularity.

And I want to ask Molly to the dance, but I can't figure out how to get those exact words to actually come out of my mouth.

And then Mr. Everett told me that eating that handful of Skittles would calm me down. But now I just feel like jumping on a trampoline with a pogo stick.

Do you have a pogo stick?

Libby Gardner

In the hallway,
clutching Trapper
Keeper tightly

8:52 a.m.

Okay, so that rumor about Corey and Trevor becoming friends? It's no rumor at all. It's true! See, I saw Corey just before homeroom. He told me that he ran into my friend Trevor. And he said he "helped him out." I had to go ahead and tell Corey my name isn't Nicole, but I've been meaning to get around to that, so the timing worked out great.

So anyway, I happen to know that "running into someone" and then "helping them out" is totally friendship. I do that all the time!

And then—get this—Corey said, "Nice skirt." To ME!

Do you know what that means?! It means if someone like Corey Long noticed it, then it's almost certain that SOMEONE is going to ask me to the dance. I just hope it's not one of the Baker twins. I have a fear of twins. They creep me out—long story, don't want to get into it. But I will say that I have an "Icky List" and twins are in my top five. No, three. Top THREE.

Okay, but the thing with Corey—it's pretty exciting. Makes me want to break out the ranch dip. I always turn to ranch dip when I'm happy. Or sad. Or cold. But only the full-fat kind—nonfat dip will not solve ANYONE'S problems.

But Trevor finding a date by the end of the day? I'm not so hopeful about that. See, that's why I'm trying to meet a lot of new girls today. I've been talking him up to convince someone cool to go with him. In fact, I already have someone in mind.

It's a lot to accomplish in one day . . . get a date for myself AND get one for Trevor too. But I just can't sit by and watch him walk straight into another stomach punch from Nancy Polanski.

CHAPTER EIGHT

TREVOR STOOD IN THE HALL WITH HIS FACE mashed on his locker door. Marty spotted him and approached with a worried look. "Trevor. I told you to chill. Face planting into your locker is *not* chilling."

Trevor looked up. "I need help, Marty. And something more than just that word."

Marty looked at his watch. "We've only been here for forty-five minutes. You need help already?"

"I need to ask that new girl Molly to the dance. By the end of the day."

"Molly? Yeah, I met that girl. She walked right up to me in the hall and asked to swap this pencil for my *Extreme Hunter* magazine. That girl loves hunting."

"She loves rare baseball cards too."

"Huh."

"Huh."

Trevor shook his head. "Listen, that's not the only problem. Libby thinks I'm going to make a bunch of friends because Corey Long was being cool to me."

"No. He's an eighth grader."

"I know."

"You can't look at an eighth grader. Or sit on an eighth grader. Much less become *friends* with one. I should know— I *am* one. And I made up that rule."

Which was true. Last year, as a seventh grader, Marty found himself on the first day of school locked in the janitor's closet without any snacks or survival gear. All because he'd asked an eighth grader if he'd step to the side so he could get a sip of water from the drinking fountain. Wilson, the janitor, found him after fifth period and fed him crackers and Easy Cheese since he'd missed lunch.

So Marty made it a rule: *If you're a seventh grader, don't look at an eighth grader or talk to one, and you might just survive the year.*

"Marty, I know Corey's an eighth grader and I should've listened to you. He tricked me into going into the teachers' bathroom."

"That was *you*?"

"Let's not—"

"Decker brought that up during announcements . . . because of *you*?"

"Can we stop with the reminders?"

"Naw, it's cool. This is my second year here, and no one's brought *me* up during morning announcements. You accomplished that in eight minutes." Marty nodded and stuck his hands in the pockets of his camouflage pants. "Impressive, dude."

The halls were chaotic with people trying to figure out how to open their lockers and push others out of the way to make room. And Marty didn't want to continue this conversation with everyone listening. It wasn't a good idea to give seventh graders the impression they could just *talk* with eighth graders. Too dangerous.

So he stepped across the hall and leaned against the wall, his foot propped up, looking like he was a casual observer, just holding up a wall. "Follow my lead," Marty explained. "We can talk, but no one can *see* us talking."

Trevor stood next to him, but not too close, and they talked quietly at each other, like secret agents in a movie when they slyly share information, typically on park benches.

"But, Libby . . ." Trevor said out of the corner of his

mouth. "She acted like she'd be impressed if I made friends with him. Plus, to get a date, she gave me a deadline." Trevor dropped his head and quietly added, "I have issues with deadlines."

Marty nodded. "You have to make them—I get it, dude. My older sister wants to be a news reporter someday; she's big on deadlines. I can help you."

Trevor wasn't sure why Marty was being so cool to him, even breaking the rules to talk to him, even if only out of the side of his mouth. But Marty seemed to understand his deadline problem and had an answer. Trevor squinted his eyes. "Help me? How?"

"We're going to kill two birds with one stone," Marty said as he glanced around and scratched at his cheek, covering up that he was talking directly to Trevor. "But not literally. Because that's impossible. I've tried. It takes at *least* two stones and usually electrical equipment."

"Okay. So I'm going to kill two birds with one stone, but not literally, because it takes more. Got it," Trevor said.

"But it's not actually two birds. It's making a friend and getting a date."

"I know!"

"So there's no manual for this sort of thing and if you were trapped in an avalanche this would be so much

easier, but if we use the techniques on page thirty-seven of *Extreme Hunter* we'll have our answer."

"But Molly has your magazine."

"Oh, that's right." Marty scratched his bald head. "I might have to wing it, then."

Marty waved him over to the drinking fountain and pretended to drink as he talked. "Here's what I'm thinking," he said in a low voice. A serious voice. A sports announcer voice. "Just like with deer, you have to ignore them to get them to come closer."

"Ignore them? That's the answer?"

"Give Molly your full attention. Ignore the guys. That way they'll wonder why you're so chill and have no choice but to think you're cool. And if *they* think you're cool, Molly will have no choice but to think you're cool—it's an association thing. And *boom!* You got yourself a date to the dance."

"That actually sounds pretty brilliant."

Marty took a moment to actually drink some water, then popped up and said, "And while you're at it, can you get my magazine back?"

"Sure. But how do I give Molly my full attention and just chill at the same time?"

Before Marty could answer, a guy with moppy brown hair sauntered up to Trevor. "Hey, I heard you're really good at Star Invaders? Is that true?"

Trevor was about to go into all the details about how to unlock certain levels and get access to online codes, but Marty's advice had luckily stuck in his head: ignore the guys, and they'll think you're cool.

"I'm Jamie," the kid said.

But Trevor looked away and folded his arms, doing his best to seem uninterested. Except instead of hanging out, basking in Trevor's obvious coolness, Jamie suddenly turned and stormed off. Why'd he get so mad? Trevor wondered.

Marty grabbed him by the shoulder. "Dude, what'd you do *that* for?"

Trevor was shocked Marty wasn't impressed. He did *exactly* what he told him to do. "I was following *your* advice. Ignore the guys."

If Marty'd had hair on his head, he would've pulled a chunk right out, so instead he slapped himself on the forehead. "Dude, that dude was a *girl*!"

"What?!"

"That was Jamie Jennison. Asking you questions. YOU! Didn't you notice her Hola! Kitty Cat! purse? And shoelaces? I mean, I know this long hair thing is confusing, but didn't you see all the other clues?"

Trevor hung his head. "I can't do this."

Marty took a deep breath and said, "Class is about to start. Hurry up and meet me inside my office."

Trevor quickly followed Marty down the hall and into the boys' bathroom.

So this is where it is! Trevor thought. Marty seemed to have the answer to everything.

Marty Nelson

Hallway, leaning
against the wall,
casually picking at
his cuticles

8:55 a.m.

Look, I didn't have much of a choice. I told Trevor
to write Molly a note. The way I see it, that's
the only way to just chill AND stalk someone at
the same time. Also because he said Libby gave him
a note. So I figure girls like things written down
or something. That's probably why Molly had that
extra pencil on her.

But I DO know Trevor can't get caught passing
notes or he'll end up in detention. I forgot to
tell him that seventh grade is different like that.
In elementary school you have to clean things if
you get in trouble. Erasers. Floors. Desks.

Not anymore. This place is severe, man.

So I taught him my signature note-passing move
. . . the trash-can dig method. It's old-school, I
know. But last year they implemented NCPAWMS . . .
No Cell Phones At Westside Middle School . . . so
we had to come up with some stealthy communication
tactics, and now we eighth graders have a duty to
pass on what we know.

Okay, so here's how it works: Get the attention of the intended receiver, approach the pencil
sharpener, then drop the note in the trash.
Intended Receiver then sharpens his/her pencil
and retrieves the note from the trash. Touchdown.

But if that doesn't work, I told him he could
always fake a sneeze and throw it at her shoe.
Because girls appreciate effort like that.

CHAPTER NINE

A COUPLE OF CLASSES LATER, **T**REVOR HAD MATH. **H**E knew Libby wouldn't be in it with him because she was in *accelerated* math and had been since kindergarten, when the class was playing with cubes and she was solving for X. To Libby, algebra was recreation.

Trevor glanced around the room and saw Molly. Perfect timing, he thought. This would give him a chance to use the advice Marty had given him. He did his best to remember it all:

Just chill.

Only pay attention to Molly.

Write her a note.

Drop it in the trash can.

Or sneeze it on her shoe.

The only problem was he never asked Marty what he should put *in* the note. Ask her where she got all her torn clothes? Ask her if she ever plans on returning the baseball card? Ask her to the dance?!

Instead of asking her anything, he just . . . wrote:

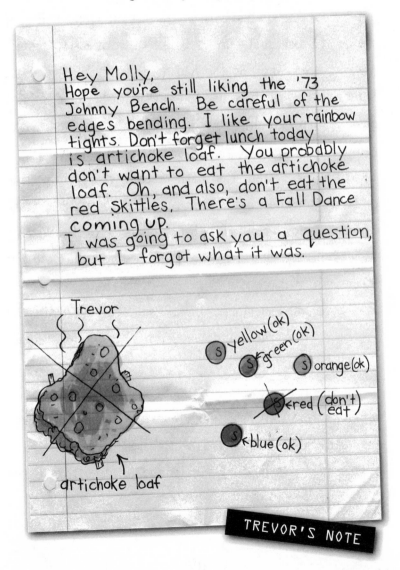

Hey Molly,
Hope you're still liking the '73 Johnny Bench. Be careful of the edges bending. I like your rainbow tights. Don't forget lunch today is artichoke loaf. You probably don't want to eat the artichoke loaf. Oh, and also, don't eat the red Skittles. There's a Fall Dance coming up.
I was going to ask you a question, but I forgot what it was.

Trevor

artichoke loaf

(S) yellow (ok)
(S) green (ok)
(S) orange (ok)
(S) red (don't eat)
(S) blue (ok)

TREVOR'S NOTE

Of course he hadn't forgotten what his question was. He just didn't know how to ask it. In a note? In person? Out *loud?!*

Trevor had gone to a dance last year, but it wasn't the type of thing where you asked a date. They all just showed up. Except Trevor had missed the e-mail Libby had sent saying it was casual—*no* ties! He had worn a tie: striped. And a blazer: wool. So she had helped him fake his great Nana's death, which he had felt bad about because she was quite a nice lady and now he couldn't let her come anywhere near his school for fear of being found out.

While Ms. Ferrell, the math teacher, was busy writing problems on the board, Trevor headed toward the trash can but tapped Molly on the shoulder as he walked by to get her attention. He wanted her to know the note was for her.

Trevor was laser-focused. *Make it to the trash can. Get this note into the hands of Mysterious Molly. Do not get detention.*

In the front row was Jason Benson, first-string third baseman from Trevor's baseball team last year. Jason cocked his head and looked up as Trevor passed his seat, noticing that Trevor was holding a note and heading toward the trash can.

Jason gave a quick nod, like he was impressed. "You know Marty too?"

"Yeah," Trevor answered. But he didn't ramble on, just kept it short.

Jason gave him a thumbs-up as he passed by. Trevor realized he had just had a brief yet successful conversation with a cool guy. First-string third baseman . . . doesn't get much better than that as far as life accomplishments go, Trevor thought. Maybe taking advice from Marty would turn out to be his best seventh grade decision yet.

But then something went wrong. Terribly wrong. His Skittles sugar buzz was wearing off. He suddenly felt sluggish, tired, *forgetful*.

Which explained why he couldn't quite remember the advice Marty had given him. He staggered toward the trash can.

What did Marty say?

Throw the note out the window?

No.

Punt it at the pencil sharpener?

No.

Sneeze the note into the trash can?

Uh, yeah. I think that's right.

Which, of course, was not right, but . . .

"Achoo!" Trevor tossed the note and it flew through the air, arched perfectly, and landed in the trash can right on top—a very precise placement.

"Gross!!!" Jason yelled out.

Trevor quickly looked up at Molly, but she was drawing on something, not paying any attention whatsoever to what was going on.

Molly . . . doodling? A serious form of perfection, he thought.

FOUND SCRIBBLED ON MOLLY'S DESK

Jason ran up to the trash can and peered in. "You just sneezed in the *trash*?"

Trevor started to explain but Ms. Ferrell charged up to them. "Boys, what's going on here?"

Jason quickly answered. "Trevor just sneezed in the trash!"

"No, I promise! I sneezed a note! I mean I—"

"Trevor, no matter where it comes from, notes are not allowed."

By this point, Jason had unraveled the paper. "This note's about a baseball card. Ha! You bring baseball cards to school?!"

"Yes. No. I mean, hidden ones, yes, but—"

"It's not his baseball card. It's mine." Molly had suddenly joined them. "And this is my note. I told him to throw it away. He was just trying to be a friend. It's my fault."

Ms. Ferrell looked over her glasses, peering down at Molly. "Then that's a—"

"I know." Molly paraded over to the teacher's desk and snatched a pink slip, then returned to her seat with a bounce in her step. Molly figured the best way to keep people from wanting to be friends was to get one of those pink slips . . . a detention slip. Because *no one* wanted to be friends with the new freaky bad kid. And getting detention on the first day was perfect bad kid behavior. Luckily for her, Trevor's note stunt had created the easiest detention-getting scenario.

Trevor watched as she happily slid back into her seat with a slight smile on her face. He pinched himself on the elbow, wondering if he was back home dreaming again.

Molly took the blame for me. She must really like me, Trevor thought.

Mysterious Molly

Emptied classroom
Sitting on teacher's
desk, swinging legs

10:49 a.m.

No, that wasn't "being friendly." That was "getting detention." It's the best way to keep people from talking to you. Plus, this place is a total bore. Detention is the most interesting part of the day. A whole hour of silence to draw? Sign me up.

But I also didn't want Trevor to get in trouble for no reason. If he has a sneezing problem, that's not for everyone else to know.

I never actually did see that note, though. I wonder if it was for me.

Nah, that's not possible. I mean, what boy would write a note to a girl and SNEEZE it in a trash can?

Unless he's getting bad advice. He sort of looks like the type of guy who isn't listening to the right people. He needs a friend. That's why I gave him that Magic 8 Ball key ring—it works just as great as a person. Maybe even better.

CHAPTER TEN

TREVOR HEADED DOWN THE HALL, VERY EXCITED ABOUT the events that had transpired in math class—well, *some* of them. But when he rounded the corner, he found himself—*wham!*—face-to-face with Corey Long.

Trevor decided he definitely needed to get that '73 Johnny Bench back from Molly *very* soon because luck was clearly not on his side.

"Looking for the bathroom again?" Corey put on his best intimidation smirk, one of the looks he practiced every morning in the visor mirror of his mom's Range Rover. She'd rate him on a scale of one to ten, and he couldn't get out of the carpool lane until he'd scored an eight or higher. "Commit to it," she'd say. Corey's mom believed confidence could be found in a dedicated smirk. She was a real estate agent.

The intimidation smirk worked because Trevor suddenly couldn't remember where he was going. "I . . . uh . . ."

"Rushing to find a seat in the cafeteria? Smart move, newbie. Just don't sit near the eighth grade section or you can say good-bye to your pizza."

Did eighth graders really not listen to things? Trevor wondered. He considered explaining to Corey that Decker had changed it to artichoke loaf, but instead decided to end the conversation there since there had been no tripping or pummeling. Trevor gingerly stepped over Corey's foot, kept his eyes straight ahead, and headed down the hallway.

Up ahead he saw the cafeteria, so he picked up the pace and quickly pushed through the doors. He remembered that Libby had mentioned in her e-mail that getting to lunch early was critical. Otherwise, all the seats would be taken and you'd end up in the hall snacking on croutons from the salad bar.

All the other students were still wandering the halls, so Trevor, alone in the cafeteria, checked out the seating possibilities, trying to guess where the eighth graders might sit. He wanted to make sure he was far, far away.

Leaning against the opposite wall was Wilson, the school janitor. He was a lean and tall man with a wrinkle-free shirt tucked tightly into his tan workpants, which were held high by a sparkling belt buckle. With a soft cloth in one hand, he polished a large tool that he held securely in his other hand. "Need something, son?" he called out across the cafeteria without looking up.

"Just checking out the seating arrangements. You're the janitor, I'm guessing?"

"Call me Wilson." He stepped away from the wall and approached Trevor. "I do custodial support, as well as many other things. But yeah. I guess you could say I'm the janitor. Just don't *call* me the janitor."

"Maybe you could give me some custodial support then? I'm trying to find a safe place to sit."

Wilson nodded. "A forward thinker. I like that."

"Yeah, most people just call me a worrier."

"Nope. You're just thinking one step ahead—that's smart. Life's a chess game. You have to come prepared."

This guy really knows what he's talking about, Trevor thought. "I need to know where the eighth graders sit. Do you know?"

"Changes every day. They like to keep the seventh graders on their toes. It's how it's always been done here. Tradition, you could say."

Trevor slumped into a nearby seat. "I'll just wait then. See where they sit when they come in." He slid his hand into the empty pocket of his backpack where the '73

Johnny Bench should've been. An empty vessel of luck.

Wilson picked up a toolbox and started toward the exit. "You'll be waiting a while. Lunch isn't for another hour." He pushed through the door and before disappearing, he added, "Be sure you're not late for class. Don't want to be the kid who gets detention on the first day."

"Dang it!" Trevor scrambled to get out of the seat and slung his backpack over his shoulder. As he bolted down the hall to get to third period on time, he realized Corey had tricked him again.

And even though Wilson seemed to have some sort of janitorial psychology degree to help with this sort of problem, Trevor knew exactly who he needed to talk to, whether they were *friend* friends or not.

So when lunchtime came around—the *real* lunchtime—Trevor immediately started his search for Libby. He needed to tell her that Corey Long—according to his squint—had very bad plans for him.

Libby would know what to do; she was magic like that. Or at least super practical.

The cafeteria quickly filled with students, and there was desperation in the air, as if everyone was in survival mode, snagging seats, running to get in line for food. The chaos made his chest hurt.

He spotted Libby already calmly seated at a table surrounded by a bunch of girls. There was still one seat open. He didn't want to alert the other girls to his Corey problem, so he knew this conversation would have to go cool, calm, and quick.

Trevor quietly and smoothly slid into the seat across from Libby. But he banged his knee on the table leg and shouted, "Ouch!!!"

She still smiled at him, seeming pleased he was sitting with their group. Trevor was relieved, so he clenched his teeth, pushing through the pain, and leaned across the table. "Lib," he said in his best cool, calm, full-of-pain whisper, "I have to tell you something."

All the girls surrounding Libby turned to look at him. But Libby didn't have time to talk with him about whatever this something was, especially not with everyone listening. So she ignored his words, sat up straight and laced her fingers together, preparing for project-ready stance. She had done her best to assemble an amazing group of girls, all date-worthy material for Trevor. Libby had spent the morning talking up his good points, with only slight bits of exaggeration, but completely understandable in her mind because it was for a good cause. The best part, Libby felt, was the fact that while secretly finding Trevor a date, she was *also* making lots of new friends, which was fantastic time management.

But the sudden spotlight on him from all these girls caused Trevor to flush with embarrassment. *Why are they all staring at me with weird grins on their faces? Do they all know about my Corey problem?*

Gossip flew fast around that school, Trevor figured, so he knew he needed to get away from all these girls before he made it any worse. He fidgeted with his napkin. "I . . . I'm going to find some guys to sit with."

"Oh." Libby was disappointed—a table full of hungry girls was the best scenario for date-asking potential. But she was the one who told him to make new friends, so how could she argue?

Trevor stood up and started to walk away, so Libby jumped up and walked next to him to give him some quick pointers. "Don't sit with the eighth graders," she instructed. "And stay away from twins."

"Why, Lib?" Trevor gave a smug look and folded his arms. He enjoyed pushing her fear-of-twins button. Sort of a hobby. "I just think it's interesting that you won't talk about your twin problem, and yet you can't stop mentioning it."

She huffed, then briskly walked away from him and over to the condiment bar.

Libby Gardner

Condiment bar
Filling many cups
with ranch dip

12:10 p.m.

Look, it was third grade. I had a crush on Fabian Fisher, all right? He was one of THEM . . . a twin.

So I wasn't as careful back then as I am now, and I ACCIDENTALLY placed a very revealing valentine into the paper bag of Frankie Fisher, not Fabian. Apparently Frankie was the type of third grader who did not often receive revealing valentines from girls. He made me rings out of blades of grass from the soccer field and followed me around for years. Yes, I said years.

No one was more excited than me when their dad got transferred to Ithaca.

NO ONE.

CHAPTER ELEVEN

TREVOR NEEDED TO FIND SOMEONE TO SIT WITH, QUICK. But finding a group of cool guys to sit with on the first day of school was a problem. Libby seemed to have very high hopes for Trevor. He spent most of his life trying not to disappoint her, along with his mother, which would explain his tendency for stomachaches.

And it would also explain the stomachache he now had as he glanced around the busy cafeteria looking for some-one—anyone—to sit with. All the while also making sure he got nowhere near Corey Long. But the seats . . . they were all nearly gone.

He carefully scanned the room and noticed two guys sitting way off in the corner, not saying very much, with one seat next to them still open. Maybe they didn't know each other and were in need of some more conversation. This could be my chance to make new friends . . . to make Libby proud, Trevor thought.

He got up enough guts, he wasn't sure from where, walked up to them and uttered the five most humiliating words in history: "Can I sit with you?"

The words came out calmly, but inside he was shaking like a Chihuahua on an iceberg.

They shrugged their shoulders.

What did shoulder shrugging mean? Trevor didn't know. But he figured it was the best offer he was going to get.

He looked them over carefully and realized they looked similar. Eerily similar. And not just same-kind-of-shirt similar . . . they had the same *faces*.

Twins.

Oh, no. Trevor worried sitting with twins would cause Libby to spiral into some post-traumatic Fear of Twins depression. But this seat was the only seat left in the *entire* cafeteria. What choice did he have?

So he slid into the chair and tried to join in on their conversation. Only they were clearly already deep into the middle of their own.

"Those are my chips."

"You took my chocolate milk."

"Mom gave it to me."

"She gave me the chips."

"Then give me the cookies."

"Not until you give me back the milk."

Trevor tried to join their argument. "Want a yogurt stick? It just reached the perfect temperature."

"Huh?" one of them asked.

Trevor was thankful for some kind of acknowledgment. But they kept staring at him—silently, blankly—like he was supposed to say something profound next. "Uh . . . the janitor is nice?"

No reaction.

He then tried to bring up the incident he'd had with the red Skittles—not a bad choice for a conversation starter. But the mere mention of food caused the twins to go right back to arguing.

"You still have my chips."

"Give me the milk."

"*After* you give me back my chips."

"Hand over the milk."

So Trevor proceeded with his safety question, the one he'd learned from Social Skills Training the counselor had given in fourth grade, the question that can never fail.

SOCIAL SKILLS TRAINING!

Need to make friends?

Question that will never fail:

Question that will always fail:

Trevor asked the name question, not the infection question, of course. There was a brief pause . . . then finally:

"Brian Baker."

"Brad Baker."

Whew. Safety question worked.

"I'm Trevor Jones," he said.

Silence.

Trevor's stomach started to hurt again. He pulled his plate closer and pushed around the artichoke loaf, which was very heavy and clearly not edible. He wondered what the lunch lady did with the leftover loaves. Did she use them for building materials? Take them home and feed them to her pet piranhas? Donate them to science? He considered posing this question to the twins, but they had already gone back to arguing about who had more chocolate chips on their cookies.

Trevor wasn't hungry anymore, and decided to head to his locker before the next class. But before he could gather his tray to leave, there was a tap at his shoulder. It was Wilson, the janitor who shall not be called the janitor. "Don't get water from the fountain," he whispered.

Trevor looked up at him. "Why?"

Wilson motioned toward the drinking fountain. "Chess

moves. Gotta think one step ahead, kid." Then he was gone.

As Trevor studied the fountain from a distance, he didn't notice anything unusual about it. So he stood up and took a few steps toward it. When his eyes fell to the floor, just in *front* of the fountain, he spotted it. A mound of mashed potatoes—rather runny—waiting to be slipped on. And just beyond that was the eighth grade seating area.

Corey Long glared at Trevor as he demonstrated a new type of intimidation smirk: the proud-of-coordinating-such-an-evil-mashed-potato-maneuver smirk. Corey had only practiced it a couple of times in the front seat of his mom's car, but he was pretty sure he nailed it.

Trevor stood frozen, realizing that Corey had placed a mound of potatoes in a strategic location on purpose, knowing that some unsuspecting kid would slip on it, and that more than likely that unsuspecting kid would be Trevor. Because really . . . who else would slip on mashed potatoes?

While Trevor stood motionless, staring at the intimidating mound, a few feet away and out of earshot Brian Baker turned to Brad Baker and said, "So that Trevor kid? I guess he's cool."

"What kid?"

"He just sat with us at lunch."

"No."

"Yes. The dude who asked us our names. You know . . . the fourth grade safety question."

"Oh, right. That guy."

"Hey, you owe me a chocolate chip cookie."

"You're wearing my shirt."

"No I'm not."

"Give it back."

"Give me my shoes."

There was a brief scuffle, which was not unusual for the Baker twins, but this time it resulted in a chocolate chip cookie soaring through the air and landing next to Trevor's foot.

Since Trevor realized Wilson had given him the heads-up and saved him from slipping on a food item, he spun out of there to get away as quickly as he could.

Which was when his left heel made contact with a squishy chocolate chip cookie that had suddenly appeared on the floor next to him. He slid and landed hard on the floor, looking as if he were trying to steal second base.

Only, this was no baseball field. It was the cafeteria floor—on the first day of school.

Brad Baker turned to Brian Baker and said, "Dude, you owe me a chocolate chip cookie."

And the cafeteria broke out in hysterics. As he scrambled to get up from the floor and wipe off his jeans, Trevor looked over at Libby. She shook her head as she bit her lip.

Libby had seen him splatter on the floor, and for an instant thought about rushing over to explain to everyone that there was a salamander on the loose and he had saved the day once again. But she knew she couldn't keep exaggerating for him forever, and eventually—she figured—he wouldn't slip on food anymore. Or at least, not quite as much.

So she turned away from him and pushed her artichoke loaf around her plate as she tried to push away the queasy feeling in her stomach.

Trevor handed the remaining intact cookie pieces back to one of the Baker twins, but as he glanced down the row, there was Molly. Staring at him. She had witnessed the entire scene. Trevor was already mortified about slipping in front of almost the entire school—for the second time that day—but his cheeks went an even deeper shade of red when he locked eyes with Molly.

Even though she was shocked by Trevor's lack of coordination, Molly had to admit she was also highly entertained by it all. She'd never seen someone have a yard sale on the cafeteria floor because of a cookie. At least not lately. Totally interesting!

Trevor knew Molly's staring must mean she was losing interest in him. *Darn. Things were going so well! How will Molly want to go to the dance with me if I constantly look like a loser?! But maybe I'm NOT one. Maybe Corey Long is FORCING me into loserdom. Yeah, that's it. I'm not the problem. Corey is.*

It was then and there that Trevor decided he needed to do something. If Libby wasn't going to fix this, he'd take matters into his own hands. A plan . . . *that* was what he needed.

And suddenly it came to him.

Trevor Jones

Outside the
cafeteria doors,
nervous pacing,
slight eye twitch

12:35 p.m.

Maybe it's not the best plan. But it can be DEFINED as "a plan." So that means I have one. Two minutes ago? No plan. Now? Plan.

See, I have to get Corey to stop harassing me, get a date, and save the world. Might as well aim high. But this plan will do just what Marty said—kill two birds with lots of stones and electrical equipment.

I call my plan . . . detention.

Did someone just laugh? Look, I know it's controversial and I probably won't ever see another Raspberry Zinger again, and maybe I should run this by my Magic 8 Ball first, but . . . I think it might be a stroke of genius.

See, this one time I was at the library and I overheard these older kids talking about this crazy loner kid who got detention on the first day of school. They seemed seriously scared of him, and also pretty respectful. That could happen to me! Getting detention on the first day of school will FORCE Corey to back off. Maybe even respect me.

This will totally work. For sure.

Now all I have to do is figure out a way to get detention.

And I have to do it before Libby convinces me it's a really bad idea and that it will give me a bad reputation. But really, at this point, ANY kind of reputation—even the worst kind—is better than none.

CHAPTER TWELVE

IT WAS TIME TO PUT THE PLAN INTO ACTION. **A**S THE BELL announcing the end of lunch rang, Trevor joined the huddled masses of kids exiting the cafeteria. There was an entire five minutes left before the next class and there was lots of wandering going on. But luckily, no Corey.

Trevor eyed Wilson as he guarded the large trash can by his supply closet. Trevor considered pushing it over and spilling it all over the hall. It would make Wilson mad and probably land him a detention. Not a bad idea. But Wilson had been helpful so far and that would be pretty cruel. Plus, trash all over the floor? Sorta gross. Trevor decided he could find a tidier way to get in trouble.

Libby snuck up behind him and tapped him on the shoulder. "Your mom keeps leaving messages on my phone."

He startled. "Mom? Why? She knows we can't have cell phones on at school."

Libby scrunched her face looking guilty. "I *may* have possibly told her she could leave me messages and I'd keep the power off. I didn't think she'd actually call, but I turned it on and look . . . four messages!"

"Why does she keep calling?"

"She's worried that you're worrying too much."

Trevor shook his head and said under his breath, "Why couldn't I have just inherited her height?"

Then he realized . . . they were alone . . . other than the hundreds of people wandering around beside them . . . and there was an *entire* five minutes available.

Trevor decided this was the perfect moment to tell her about Corey—that he was evil and was trying to ruin him. However, before he could start forming the words, Libby distracted him as she looked up at a poster on the wall.

It was a poster that explained things that could land a student in detention. But part of it had been scratched through with a marker. Who would vandalize a detention poster? Trevor leaned in, trying to decipher what number three said, but Libby grabbed his arm. "We have to get to class."

"Wait, Lib. I need to tell you something." Trevor pushed his back against the wall, trying to get out of the way of

Ways to Earn a Detention:

1. Using a cell phone

2. Upsetting Wilson

3. ▰▰▰▰▰▰▰▰▰▰▰

the groups of people pushing past them, all glued at the hips, it seemed. "See . . . the thing about Corey—"

Libby's cell phone chirped; her ringtone was set to Blue Jay. The sound filled the hallway like an alarm, causing people to turn and look at them. The two of them snapped their heads up, studying each other with waffle-sized eyes. They both had seen the poster and knew that a chirping cell phone meant one thing for sure: if a teacher heard it . . . detention!

"We're not allowed to use phones at school. It's one of the top two ways to earn a detention!" Libby whisper-yelled. She glanced down at the screen. "But it's your mom again!"

"You'll get in trouble," Trevor said, faking his helpfulness. "Hand it to me. I'll answer it."

"No, you'll get detention. I'll turn it off."

He casually took it out of her hand. "But you know my mom—she must be calling about something important."

"A detention is the *last* thing you want. It goes on your permanent record!" Libby grabbed the phone back.

"Let me answer it," he pleaded.

More and more students started to turn their heads at the bird chirping sound.

Libby quickly pushed the green *on* button and cupped her hand around the phone as she whispered. "Hi, Ms. Jones? Yeah, it's going great. Trevor's close to becoming friends with a really cool guy. But we can't talk—"

Trevor glared her down and eyebrowed as loud as he

could, *No! Stop!* Because now he was going to have to make a new friend to impress his *mother,* too!

As Trevor looked up through the crowd, he could see Mr. Everett walking toward them. *Trevor* was the one who needed to get a detention, not Libby.

So he reached for her phone. "Let me talk."

Libby hesitantly handed it over. "It's your mom."

"I *know*!" He stepped away from Libby so she couldn't hear. "Mom? Yes, I'm getting along with my peers. No, I'm not exactly friends with a cool guy yet. Of course I respect you. . . . No, I didn't realize you had me through natural childbirth. . . . Yes, I realize you want me to live up to my highest potential. . . . No, I didn't know that. . . ."

Ever since his parents divorced a few years ago, Trevor had received a daily lecture from Ms. Jones on being a good person, living up to his potential, respecting girls, et cetera.

Trevor was pretty sure it had something to do with his dad's decision to move away from them to the beach and become a professional surfboard shaper. And also the owner of a beat-up VW van with a bad paint job.

That didn't sound so awful to Trevor, but regardless, it resulted in daily reminders from his mom to *not* disappoint people.

Just as Mr. Everett walked up, Trevor said, "Hang on," and cupped his hand over the tiny receiver so his mom couldn't hear. "Yes, Mr. Everett?" Trevor couldn't help but beam. His plan was working.

"You are not allowed to use cell phones on campus. That's a detention."

Trevor popped up nice and tall. "Detention? You want to give *me* detention?! Then, yes! I am definitely using a cell phone. Look at this, Mr. Everett!" Trevor held it close to the side of his head while still covering the receiver. "I am definitely using a cell phone!"

Libby looked at him, horrified. She couldn't believe it. Was he actually *trying* to get detention? Did he not know what that would do to his reputation? It would shrink his pool of possible dates to practically zero. No girl would want to get asked by some jerk who gets detention on the first day. Probably not even Nancy Polanski.

And even though he didn't aspire to it, he'd never be able to run for public office, something Libby was all too familiar with, since she had memorized the student council president requirements. Because, of course, *this* would be the year she'd take the title back from Cindy.

"Hand the phone over, Trevor," Mr. Everett insisted as he squinted his eyes at him. Mr. Everett grabbed the little pink phone and held it up to his ear. "Hello? . . . Oh! Ms. Jones! So lovely to talk to you. . . . No, I didn't realize there was a community fund-raiser this weekend. . . . Yes, of course I'll help. . . . No, I didn't realize you gave birth naturally. . . . Okay, see you then. . . . I'll be sure to tell him. Bye, Ms. Jones."

Mr. Everett handed the phone back to Trevor. "Try to live up to your potential, Trevor. Don't be a disappointment."

"What about detention?"

"As long as you respect your mother, you're off the hook." Mr. Everett walked away whistling.

Oh, man. How hard is it to get a measly detention around here?

Libby charged up to him. "You did *not* just try to get a detention, did you? Do you know how hard that would make it for me to find you a date?"

"I was just trying to—" But then her words finally landed on the comprehension part of his brain. "Wait. It would make it hard for you to . . . *what*?" Trevor stepped back. *Did she say she's finding a date for me?* He stuffed his hands in his pockets and rocked from foot to foot, feeling relieved that Libby was back to being in charge of his social life again.

Libby chewed at her cuticle, trying to figure her way out of this one. "I *said* how hard it would be for *you* to find a date. Why would I find you a date? That's ridiculous." She threw her hands up in an exasperated manner, hoping this would distract him and he'd stop thinking about the whole thing. "Just get to class on time, Trevor."

Trevor didn't really know what to think, because all her hand flailing was very distracting. And also he could've sworn she said she was finding him a date. But it ended up he didn't have time for thinking much more about this anyway, because as Libby walked away and the hallway crowd started to disperse, he saw one person still lingering.

Corey Long, leaning against a locker, mentally controlling the room temperature, reeking of coolness. Like always.

Corey Long

Using drumsticks on his locker to tap out an impressive rhythm, clearly in another league

12:55 p.m.

Yeah, this next thing is part of the tradition too. A dude sends you to the wrong bathroom, you get tripped, and then you get reminded of it all day. It's nothing personal. Just business.

And Trevor might even be sorta cool. He was talking on a cell phone and that is totally detention-worthy behavior.

It's like that scene in that mutant ninja turtle movie. The one where the guy . . . does that thing . . . I can't remember. Whatever. But Leonardo is the coolest. I'm totally Leonardo.

Or, no. Maybe I'm Splinter, the rat—their master.

[impressive finale drumroll, then stuffs his drumsticks in his backpack and fixes hair so it falls over his eyes]

Yeah. I'm the rat.

CHAPTER THIRTEEN

TREVOR DIDN'T KNOW WHAT TO DO. **RUN? FAKE A** stomachache? *Run?*

Without realizing it, Trevor tilted his eyebrows as he stared Corey down. Good thing it wasn't Libby standing there because an eyebrow tilt like that one meant, "Want to play video games?" He rubbed his brows and immediately changed them back to a neutral tilt.

Corey didn't eyebrow anything back. But he *did* send him a message: he pointed down to his foot, the exact same one that had tripped Trevor not just a few hours before, then tapped it on the floor. Clearly, an evilness tap. And he topped it off with a shifty smile.

Trevor knew he was being reminded of his utter embarrassment. He knew Corey had every intention of humiliating him until old age. And he knew he needed to get to class on time.

So did everyone else, apparently, which explained why the hall had suddenly cleared. And there they were, the two of them—Trevor and Corey—all alone.

Trevor waited for the duel music to start, but instead Corey sauntered over to him. Trevor flinched.

FOUND IN TREVOR'S NOTEBOOK

And this made Corey laugh. "I'm not going to trip you, dude. Don't have to. Rumors fly fast around here. All I have to do is tell that Cindy girl you were flat on your back, and everyone will believe it."

Trevor shrugged, trying his best to act like the threat of a tripping rumor didn't bother him.

"Everyone will believe it—even that Molly girl." Corey started to walk away, but turned back. "I hear she's hoping someone *cool* will ask her to the dance, not some dude who gets tripped in the hall all day. Too bad rumors fly fast, huh?"

Why was Corey doing this? And how did he know Molly? Trevor decided maybe it was time to stand up to this guy. "That's where you're wrong, Corey. She *doesn't* want someone cool to ask her to the dance."

And *that* came out wrong.

But before he could figure out the right thing to say, Corey was gone.

Corey Long

Sipping water from
the hall fountain

Late, but totally
not worried about
it

1:01 p.m.

Yeah, I probably took that one too far. But did
you see the way the crowd disappeared? And how I
had to face him alone? It was like that scene in
Raiders of the Lost Ark where . . . no, wait . . .
maybe it was *The Temple of Doom*. Sheesh, I don't
know. But it was an intense scene.

So I had to say SOMETHING. I've got a reputation. It takes work to keep this thing going. I
mean, I didn't get to be legendary at this school
by doing my own homework and enjoying the school
lunches. No. Reputations take commitment!

Like in *Toy Story*. Those little dudes never
give up.

Who, me? I guess if I had to choose I'd be Buzz
Lightyear. Woody's sorta wimpy, you know?

Or maybe that pig? He's funny.

Yeah. I'm the pig.

When Trevor got to P.E., he saw his class was sharing the blacktop with an eighth grade class. Fortunately he recognized one of them: Marty.

He leaned over from his line and got Marty's attention. "Psst. I have to ask you something."

"We shouldn't be talking," Marty said out of the corner of his mouth.

"I know," Trevor whispered. "But number three was crossed out on that poster and I need to know how to get detention."

Marty tilted his head. "Don't know. I've never gotten detention."

"You? Really?"

"Just because I shave my head doesn't mean I torture cats for fun or something."

"Really?"

"No. I hunt and kill things for *sport*."

"Oh. That's . . . better."

Marty looked left, then right, making sure no one was paying attention, then leaned in closer. "Look, I've heard there is *one* way you can get detention."

"Passing notes?"

"You mean getting *caught* passing notes. There's a fine distinction. And I would never give you advice if I thought you'd get caught passing one. You didn't get caught, right?"

Trevor tried to block the memory from his mind. The one where he was spotted in math class sneezing a note in the trash can.

"Me?" Trevor waved him off. "Pfft. Naw."

"Okay, so I'll let you in on what I know." He lowered his voice. "Be late for class."

"That's it? Be late? But that's so easy."

"No one said this detention thing would be hard."

Trevor shrugged. "Your sources are probably the best."

Marty started to walk off but turned back. "Hey, you never told me why you're trying to get detention."

Trevor considered telling him the truth about his big master plan, about getting detention so Corey would think he was bad and back off.

But by the time all these thoughts ran through Trevor's head, Marty had become bored and wandered off to give tips to a group of kids playing dodgeball on how to aim perfectly at their prey.

So Trevor glanced at his schedule card to see what his next class was. Science. Mr. Everett.

He decided for the first time in his life he would be late, and even though technically he had been late for homeroom that morning, this time would be different . . .

he would get *caught*. And Mr. Everett would have to hand over that elusive pink slip.

He walked over and leaned against the brick wall, giving himself a pep talk about being late. *You can do this. You can break a rule if it's for the good of mankind. Or at least for the good of your social life. You don't want to end up with a stomach punch from Nancy Polanski and have to drink Slurpees alone at the 7-Eleven on prom night. Libby would not be impressed. And Mom would be disappointed; she's had enough of guys who don't live up to their potential. I'm not going to be that guy.*

He took a deep satisfied breath. But suddenly he realized a pep talk near a game of dodgeball was not a good idea.

Marty Nelson

Bouncing a rubber
ball against a
brick wall

2:03 p.m.

I never said I had good aim. And I apologized to
Trevor. It only left a little mark. He's cool . . .
we're cool.

So that thing about how to get detention I
heard from this girl, Cindy Applegate. I'm not
sure why she told me. She seemed to like talking
a lot. And she kept standing there twirling in her
skirt, like she was waiting for something. Like I
was supposed to ask her something? So I kept asking her questions hoping I'd ask the right one.

I'm not sure I've done it yet.

Cindy Applegate

At her locker mirror

Chewing gum,
applying bubble
gum—flavored
lip gloss

2:07 p.m.

Okay, get this. So that Marty guy? He keeps asking me questions and then he waits and stands there and waits and then asks me another one.

I think that's called "a crush." I'm guessing he wants to ask me to the dance. That must be why he's asking me so many questions. He figures he'll ask a lot of questions then pop the big one and I'll say yes.

Will I? Oh, I don't know. I don't even know him yet. So that's why I told him I had to leave or else I'd get detention for being late to class. Which isn't even true. They don't count you late until next week. Everyone knows that.

But I'm guessing Trevor will ask me to the dance too. He was doing all that nervous dancing around in the hall earlier. And probably Corey will ask me. I mean, he had his friend carry my backpack. So sweet! And then there are those twins. I noticed those two have been arguing all day, CLEARLY about which one was going to ask me to the dance. Right? I mean what else would twins argue about?

But this day is almost over. I'm sure someone will ask me soon. I've gone through three whole packs of gum today—I chew gum when I'm super hopeful.

CHAPTER FOURTEEN

TREVOR PACED AROUND OUTSIDE THE CLASSROOM, THEN peeked in. Lots of students, but no Mr. Everett yet. So he paced the hall some more. He pretended to sip water at the fountain. He picked up invisible pieces of trash. He even straightened some of the artwork in the hallway. Anything to eat the time and keep him busy until that late bell rang.

But as the seconds ticked by and he knew he was getting closer and closer to being late, his palms went clammy. Then sweat beads formed on his forehead. His brain did that excessive questioning thing:

What am I doing? Is it worth all this to get detention? Just to get Corey off my back? But there's no way Molly will ever go to the dance with me if Corey is constantly making me look like a loser.

He glanced down the hall. Molly was heading into her class. Their eyes briefly met. And just before she disappeared into the room, she smiled at him.

FOUND IN TREVOR'S NOTEBOOK

Slight, but still a smile

Yep. Totally willing to get detention.

Three, two, one . . . riiiiiing!

And in that instant, Trevor's life story had been altered.

He could never again say he had made it to everything on time. That chapter in his life was over.

Trevor took a deep breath, willing to accept the consequences of his lateness. Even though he knew it meant dealing with his mother. But people forgiving people and still feeding them snacks is a very common occurrence.

"Trevor!" Mr. Everett was barreling down the hall, followed closely by Wilson. This was quite unlike Mr. Everett, given that his comfortable shoes were for casual walking. Not *barreling*. "This is a problem!" he yelled out.

Trevor stuck his palm out and waited to be handed the pink detention slip. "Sorry for being late. I can't believe you have to give me detention. But I understand."

Mr. Everett reached into his pocket, but instead of a detention slip he pulled out a handful of Skittles. "*This* is the problem. No reds. They're all gone."

"I only ate three earlier today, I promise."

"I know I had exactly forty-seven red ones left. This is highly unusual. I lose a lot of things, but *all* the red Skittles?"

Trevor tried to get back to the issue at hand—namely his entire future social life. "Anyway? About me being late? I know you have to give me detention—"

"Trevor." Mr. Everett lowered his voice. "You can't get

detention for being late during the first week of school. Everyone knows that."

"Everyone. Of course they do." Trevor lowered his head and scuffled into the classroom, then took his seat. Marty said this getting detention thing wouldn't be hard . . . for everyone but Trevor, it seemed.

Mr. Everett immediately got the class's attention. "Something terrible has happened. My red Skittles are missing. So while I'm tearing this school apart, brick by brick, you are going to take a field trip out to the hall with Wilson, the man in charge of custodial support. He's going to give you a lesson on proper locker etiquette."

The students all grumbled and headed out of the class.

In the middle of the hall was Wilson standing with his hands behind his back, chin held high, with excellent posture. He waited for the class to crowd around him, then cleared his throat.

"The reason why I'm here speaking to you today is because of this." He held up his hand. "In my right hand is where you will always find Lefty, my commercial-grade locker de-jamming tool. You're looking at genuine titanium special ordered from a factory in Pittsburgh. Getting my initials carved in the handle may have been a little over the top, but this is no ordinary tool. Lefty here will help you get your locker open should you happen to get it jammed shut with papers and books and detention slips."

Trevor looked around; everyone was nodding. *Really? Getting a locker jammed with detention slips is a common occurrence? Why is it so hard for me to get one measly slip?!*

"Locker jamming may not sound scary to you," Wilson continued, "but the truth is three out of four kids experience serious locker jamming situations at some point during their middle school careers that require the use of a locker de-jamming tool. Without Lefty, this school would come to a screeching halt—we couldn't function without it."

The students were amazed by all that went into properly securing a locker door without getting it jammed. And also amazed by Wilson's passion for locker de-jamming. They were witnessing a man who had found his calling in life.

Given that Trevor had made friends with the janitor at their elementary school, he knew that janitors not only had amazing floor-buffing equipment, but also knowledge of all things school-related—the rules, the inner workings, the *real* story.

Wilson was the person he needed to help him get detention. He'd know for sure what had been scratched out on the bottom of that poster.

Wilson

In charge of custodial support

Leaning against supply closet, buffing out finger smudges on the handle of his tool

2:20 p.m.

We were in negotiations once to do a feature article on me in *Janitorial Weekly*. But it never materialized—an "editorial disagreement."

What kind? Let's just say we had a difference of opinion on wording. It's a Supply Containment Unit, *NOT* a janitor's closet. They found someone else to write the article. So forget the publishing world. I can change lives right here at Westside Middle School.

You see, these kids here . . . they don't seem to understand how important posture is when it comes to opening and closing a locker door. You can't secure a latch properly without your shoulders back and your feet firmly planted shoulder-width apart. Without it, you have the outbreak of locker jammings we've seen. It's reaching epidemic proportions.

But kids these days are all hunched over. No posture! Could be heavy backpacks, or lack of vitamin C, or crummy attitudes. And that new kid, Trevor? Good kid, but like I said, hunched over. I don't think he has a vitamin C problem; he might just be getting the wrong advice.

Now, do NOT get me started on the overflowing trash situation in the cafeteria. Proper spine alignment is the only answer, but I can't fix every problem.

I'm just one man. One mission at a time.

Wilson spent the rest of the period demonstrating proper locker opening technique along with good posture. When the bell rang, kids spilled out of the classrooms and Libby snuck up next to Trevor.

"I know I'm not in charge of your life anymore, but I heard you were late for class."

Trevor was almost impressed with the rate gossip spread in this school. And since that was the case, there was no sense in denying it. "Yes. I was late."

"You know starting next week that counts as a detention."

"I do *now*."

She squinted her eyes at him. "Wait. You were *trying* to get detention, weren't you?"

He couldn't tell her the truth. She'd never let him go through with actually getting a detention. She'd probably haul him over to Mr. Everett and explain to him that Trevor had restless leg syndrome that caused him to be late to class, and any detentions would be a violation of his rights. He'd probably get a free bag of Skittles and Mr. Everett's pity—which was tempting.

But it wasn't part of the plan. He'd have to go through with keeping his detention scheme a secret from Libby and just hope for mercy later. "Me, *trying* to get a detention?

No! I was held up because of . . . a *lot* of trash . . . on the floor . . . it was in my way." Trevor was not quite as experienced as Libby in the act of covering things up.

She held her squint. Then finally released. "Okay, good."

But Trevor needed to get back to the important stuff. "Libby?"

"Yeah?"

"So you're saying you're *not* in charge of my life anymore?"

"Do you want me to be?"

Of course, that would be helpful, Trevor thought. Someone else in charge? Never having to make his own decisions? Life going back to how it used to be? Of course!

But then again, maybe that wasn't such a good idea. She wanted him to make changes. Stop looking at baseball cards. Stop ~~doodling~~ drawing. Become friends with guys like Corey Long. And Trevor didn't want any of these things.

So Trevor stood up tall—just like Wilson had taught them—and said, "I need to tell you the truth."

"Wait." Libby fidgeted with her skirt. "I have to tell you something."

He winced and braced for the truth. Whatever her truth was, he figured it was probably going to be much different from his.

"Remember that deadline I gave you that you had to ask a date to the Fall Dance by the end of the day?" She checked her watch. "I hate to break it to you, but we only have one more class left. You have fifty-four minutes."

Only one more class left to ask Molly? Trevor suddenly felt dizzy.

Libby noticed Trevor bracing the wall. "But you don't have to worry about it," she said with lots of pep, trying to be encouraging. "All you have to do is find some girl in class, maybe someone sitting next to you, and ask her. Simple!"

Libby had big plans for those final fifty-four minutes. True, she had come *way* too close to the deadline, but this had proven to be a difficult task. Because even though she had gotten plenty of girls interested in Trevor, for some reason he kept ignoring them. Just nerves, she figured.

This project was definitely the hardest Libby had taken on, but she knew she could still make it work. Libby's plan was to sit next to Jamie Jennison. Then, just as Trevor entered the room, she'd fake a headache. She could easily claim the fluorescent lighting at the front of the room was causing a migraine and she'd have to move to the back (much better lighting) with Trevor taking her seat. Trevor would chat with Jamie, he'd look at the clock, his deadline disorder would kick in—and *whammo!*—he'd ask the question. She'd say yes, and his entire future social life would be fixed. Easy. She hoped it would turn out just as easy for her to get a date for herself too.

"Trevor, say something."

Trevor stared blankly at Libby, wondering if he should tell her he already planned on asking Molly. "Don't worry, Lib. I'll ask *someone* by the end of the day."

A big, satisfied smile filled her face.

Trevor looked at his schedule card. His last class of the day was language arts. "What's your last class?" he asked her.

Libby checked hers, acting as if she didn't already know they'd be in the same class. "Oh, language arts!"

"Cool," Trevor said. "I'll see you in there. But I promise not to talk to you or sit near you or use your name out loud in any way."

Libby lightly punched him on the shoulder. "Thanks, Trev," she said, then headed down the hall ahead of him.

He slowly scuffled toward the last class of the day with dread in every step. Only one class left to get detention, make Corey back off, and ask Molly to the dance. That was a lot to ask of the next fifty-two minutes. It seemed impossible.

Only an act of unforeseen miraculousness could fix this, which would be extremely rare. But luck must have suddenly decided to side with Trevor Jones, because something extremely rare was *exactly* what happened.

CHAPTER FIFTEEN

WHEN **TREVOR** ENTERED THE ROOM, HE LOOKED around, hoping to find Molly, but she wasn't there. He wasn't going to make his deadline.

Libby was sitting in the front row and strangely, without warning, she jumped up out of her seat and marched up to Trevor with her hand on her forehead. Why was she coming to talk to *him*? "Amnesia?" he asked.

"Headache," she said in a weak voice. "Those lights . . . too fluorescent . . ." She motioned with her other hand to her now empty seat. "Take mine." She patted him on the back.

"Sure, Lib," he said reluctantly. He never did like the front row; everyone could see your every move. He slowly approached, and once he got to the desk, realized it was a very bad idea. Because sitting in the seat to the left was Jamie Jennison, the girl he'd thought was a guy. And in the chair to the right was Jake Jacobs, the guy he'd thought was a girl. This was bound to turn into a humiliating event of monumental proportions.

He started to turn and beg Libby to take her seat back, but fortunately he didn't have to. It was at that moment that the extremely rare event occurred.

The intercom crackled. "Students," Vice Principal Decker said. "I have an announcement."

Wilson

Digging around in his Supply Containment Unit
Visibly shaken

2:45 p.m.

Yes, I realize I am visibly shaken. According to the Janitorial Code of Behavior, I'm required to stay calm in emergencies like these.

This could simply be a false alarm, but it appears to be a dire situation . . . LEFTY IS MISSING.

I do not want to jump to any conclusions. I'm not going to haul everyone into the gym and interrogate them or anything. No, I'm simply going to retrace my steps.

I may have placed it in my Containment Unit. Or set it down next to a severely jammed locker. There's a reasonable explanation. And I'm going to find out what it is.

"Listen up, you pipsqueaks!" Wilson yelled.

Wilson had made Decker call a rare emergency all-school assembly, and the entire school was hustled into the gym.

Wilson paced in front of the crowd like a lion in a midsized town zoo—very anxious. Vice Principal Decker approached Wilson and whispered to him so he couldn't be heard over the microphone, except he *could*. "You can't actually call them pipsqueaks."

"Fine." Wilson tightened his grip on the microphone as he paced back and forth on the foul line. "Some *turkey* here has stolen my locker tool!"

The crowd gasped. Even the new seventh graders knew not to mess with a janitor's tools.

Vice Principal Decker leaned over again. "You can't actually *accuse* them of anything. Or call them names. Especially not animal names."

Wilson cupped his hand over the microphone. "You mean I'm supposed to be *nice* to them?"

Vice Principal Decker nodded.

Wilson cleared his throat. "Listen up, you wonderfully enchanting young adults. It appears a magical fairy has hidden my tool and I need your help." Wilson smiled but his teeth were clenched. What he really wanted to do was interrogate each and every student—with techniques

approved by the Janitorial Code of Behavior, of course—until he found the culprit. But the list of approved interrogation techniques was very short. He shook his head, frustrated by the words he was about to speak. "How about we make an anonymous tip box?"

Wilson looked back at Vice Principal Decker. Decker was nodding energetically, apparently very supportive of this nonforceful, non-name-calling anonymous tip box idea.

Trevor was sitting in the back row. That was because when the emergency assembly was called, he decided to take advantage of the miraculous moment and sit next to Molly. He saw her at the top of the bleachers, doodling, so he climbed the steps and sat in the open seat next to her. He nodded at her. She nodded at him. It was a good start.

Trevor figured he would go ahead and ask Molly to the dance right then and there. All he had to do was get the right words to come out of his mouth. After all, people thinking of the right words is a very common occurrence, Trevor reminded himself.

As Wilson explained how to write anonymous tips, Trevor leaned over to Molly. "Can I ask you a question?"

"An anonymous tip means you don't have to write your name," she answered, without looking at him.

"No, that's not what—"

"Okay, this day was interesting for like a second, but not anymore. I'm gone." Molly jumped up. "See ya, Trevor." And she casually walked off the bleachers and out the exit.

Wow, you can just do that? Leave school before the dismissal bell rings? Wasn't she worried Decker would stop her? Didn't they have rules at her other school? Trevor had never met a girl quite so unaware of the rules, and he had to admit it made her even more interesting. But it also made it *impossible* to ask her to a dance.

"One more thing." Vice Principal Decker grabbed the microphone. "Now, I'm not accusing anyone of stealing, but if someone did take the tool—and no one is saying that anyone did—but if I *had* to punish someone—and no one is saying any student will get punished, especially since we're fully aware it could have been a magical fairy as Wilson suggested—but—BUT!—if I *did* have to punish a student and/or fairy who stole the tool"—Vice Principal Decker waved his stack of pink slips—"it would be a detention."

Pink slips? Trevor suddenly remembered Molly snatching one of those off the teacher's desk in math class. Molly wasn't leaving school; she was heading to detention. And that's where he could ask her!

Trevor decided he would break rule number two on that poster—as much as he wished there were another way—and he would get detention by upsetting Wilson.

He raised his hand.

Wilson shielded his eyes from the fluorescent lighting as he spotted Trevor's hand. "Yes? In the back. Trevor?"

Everyone turned and glared at him, clearly shocked that the janitor knew him *by name* on the first day of school.

But he didn't let the glares bother him; he simply cleared his throat and said in a loud, strong voice, "I'm the one who took your locker tool."

Except the glares *did* bother him, so that's not at all what came out of Trevor's mouth. What *actually* came out was:

"   ."

Apparently saying the right words was not a common occurrence for Trevor. And in this moment, neither was saying *any* words.

Wilson tapped his finger on his silver belt buckle. "Did you want to say something, son?"

"I—I . . ." He spotted Libby two rows away, her eyes fixed on him. "I'll help make the anonymous tip box." Trevor dropped his head, bummed that he hadn't gone through with it.

161

The bell rang and everyone was dismissed. It was the end of the day.

Wait. He didn't get detention. The day was over!

Trevor had missed his deadline and now he'd have to deal with a disappointed best friend and a future social life filled with no prom and a lonely night with Slurpees. He stumbled back to his locker, dragging his feet, head dangling. So it was at that point that he went back to doing what he did best so far in seventh grade.

"Were you going to ask me a question?" Molly had walked up behind him.

He turned to face her and immediately covered his forehead, aware of the red mark that was probably forming due to his locker face-plant. "Uh . . . I—I—" *Come on, right words. Form!* "Has anyone asked you to the dance?"

She shrugged, the same interesting shrug she'd done earlier. "Yeah."

Trevor swallowed hard. Who would've asked her?

"But I told him no," she added.

His shoulders slumped in relief. Trevor could breathe again. Whew. Time to ask the question.

"Trevor!" Wilson marched up and shoved a box of markers in his hand. "I appreciate your making that anonymous tip box for me. We have to find this pipsqueak turkey. Do *not* tell Decker I said that."

"Sure, Wilson." But when Trevor turned back to ask Molly his question, she was gone. He slumped again, but this time it was a frustration slump.

Wilson slapped him on the back as he walked on. "And stand up straight, kid. Your posture is horrendous."

He pushed his shoulders back and stood up, just like Wilson said. And then . . . it worked! It was probably the additional oxygen flowing through his now-straight spine and getting to his brain, because Trevor suddenly realized Marty *had* been right about one thing . . . writing notes. Marty had told him writing notes wouldn't get him detention . . . but getting *caught* would. That was how Molly had gotten a detention, when she took the blame for his writing that note.

Trevor hustled down the hall and saw that the door to the detention room was still open. He angled himself so that he could see Miss Plimp, school counselor, as she wrote the detention rules on the board. Molly was doodling on her paper.

She didn't just doodle, she doodled *all the time.*

Some sort of total complete perfection, he thought.

He ripped out a piece of notebook paper and quickly wrote a note in large letters.

Molly, will you go to the dance with me?

He looked it over and nodded with certainty. But then he was suddenly attacked with doubt. What if she said no? What if she didn't even remember talking to him earlier? What if she needed glasses and couldn't read a note from this far away?

Trevor decided to stick with his *safer* version of the Get Detention Plan. He would simply get caught with a note. He would get detention. He would sit next to Molly. He would ask her to the dance. Safer is always better, he told himself.

So he flipped the paper over and wrote a *different* note in large letters.

My name is Trevor Jones. This is a note.

Miss Plimp finished her list of rules, and Trevor flipped the note up and stood with his feet planted shoulder-width apart—very close to appropriate locker door opening stance—and held his note up high for all to see. He winced as he prepared for the consequences.

Miss Plimp tilted her head and looked out the door. She squinted as she looked his way, then let out a big sigh. A sure indication of disappointment, which was sure to be followed by a pink slip.

Trevor stood strong with his note high in the air as Miss Plimp took three steps closer to him and planted her hands on her hip. "Trevor Jones!"

The whole detention class—including Molly—looked up to see what was going on.

Oh, finally, he thought. Why didn't I just do this earlier? So easy!

"Trevor, close that door!"

"But I'm holding a—"

"There's a draft!" she added. But she didn't wait for Trevor to close the door. She marched over and reached out to close it herself.

He glanced down at his note and when he saw what he had done his stomach fell to the floor. He had held up the wrong side. He was showing the other side—the side that asked Molly to the dance.

Oh, no! Did anyone see it?

But just as Miss Plimp closed the door and it slowly started to creak shut, he glanced up and caught Molly's eye. Oh, yes indeed, she had seen the entire thing. And she was holding up her paper for him to see. On it she had written one word, in very big letters, with an exclamation point and everything.

CHAPTEЯ SIXTEEN

TREVOR HUSTLED OVER TO THE BUS AND JUMPED ON just in time before it took off. But his stomach dropped when he saw the bus was completely full. He remembered how not-so-great the morning bus ride had gone when he'd sat on an eighth grade foot.

"Trevor!"

He saw a hand waving to him from near the back. It was Libby. And she had saved the last seat for him. He was shocked that she actually wanted to sit next to him for all the public to see. What is this about? he wondered. Talking—that's what. She wants a full report.

He decided it would be best to go ahead and tell her absolutely everything—that Corey was pretty much evil and trying to ruin him and the odds of making a new friend were slim to none with Corey alive and breathing on this planet, but that he had *still* managed to get a date on deadline, which deserved an award or maybe one of those standing ovations, or at least a bobblehead trophy.

But when he slid into the seat and looked her over, he realized she was nervous about something.

FOUND IN TREVOR'S NOTEBOOK

TWIRL

CHEW

Nervous behavior, right?

He wasn't sure this was the right time to talk to her, but he never seemed to know when the right time was anyway, so he blurted it all out at once. "I did get a date to the dance but I'm pretty sure that Corey Long is out to get me, so I'm not totally sure this becoming his friend thing is going to work out because—"

"You got a date?" Libby skipped right over the Corey part.

"Yep."

She released all of her strands of hair and clasped her hands together tightly. "A date to the dance. We're talking about the *dance*, right?" She couldn't believe it. Even with the disaster that had occurred, with Wilson calling an emergency assembly and thwarting her plans, Trevor *still* managed to ask Jamie? Awesome!

"Yes, Libby. Molly wrote *yes* in big letters and the paper was aimed right at me."

Libby couldn't believe what she was hearing. "Wait. You asked Molly? *New girl* Molly?!"

"Your questions seem more like opinions," Trevor said, even though he had to admit he was a little shocked Molly had said yes, too. Was it the baseball card? Because other than giving her the card, he had made an absolute fool of himself the rest of the day. He figured maybe time had run out for Molly too, and she had to say yes to *someone*. Whatever the reason, it didn't really matter—he'd met his deadline.

Libby fiddled with the hem of her skirt, stalling while she dealt with her feelings of shock. How could he have messed this up? *Molly?!* She'd told him—very clearly, as always—exactly what he needed to do: ask a cool girl. Someone nice, decently dressed, with some sort of personality, the type of girl who would improve his chances of better dates in the future. Not someone who would improve his chances of ending up in juvenile hall.

But Libby was the one who had put Trevor up to this; he'd only done what she'd told him to do. She just didn't know she'd have to specify *not* to pick a girl who was ripped and striped and who she could only guess was a serial detention-attender. She and Trevor weren't *friend* friends, but she was still his friend. So she decided to be supportive. "Molly. That's great. Perfect choice." She clutched her stomach. "Molly's mysterious and new and striped and ripped. What's not to like? That makes her *so* . . . you know . . . interesting."

Trevor noted Libby was suddenly using lots of words, directed at him—something she hadn't done all day. Why was the subject of Molly suddenly making her ultra-talkative?

Trevor figured excessive chatter meant she didn't want to talk about the *real* problem: herself. She was clearly worried about her own date. And this amount of nervousness could only mean one thing. "Did a twin ask you to the dance?"

"Nope."

"Jason? Jake?"

She looked out the bus window. "No. And no."

Huh. Trevor wasn't sure who else to guess. "Marty?"

"No! And he asked Cindy anyway."

Strange pairing, Trevor thought. But then he realized what Libby's fidgeting and the chattering was all about—she didn't get asked at all. "I'm sorry, Lib. I can't believe you're not going to the dance."

"Oh, I'm going. I got asked right before school ended."

"You did? Who?"

Her knees started bouncing and she gave a huge grin, one that she had been holding in for longer than she wanted. Because even though she knew that her choice in denim skirt would result in landing a date, she hadn't imagined it would land her a date *this* cool. "Corey Long!!" she blurted.

Trevor couldn't believe what he was hearing. "Wait. Corey? We're talking about Corey *Long*, right?"

Her face dropped. "What's wrong?"

"Are you sure that was a smart decision? I mean, you have lots of options. Right?"

She huffed. "Sounds like *you're* the one with the opinion now."

Of *course* he had an opinion. Corey Long was out to get him. He was the worst choice in dates in the history of date choices *ever*. But then again, Libby had put so much thought into this day, what with the pressed skirt and all. How could he ruin it for her? As much as it made his stomach ache, he was her friend, which meant he'd have to be . . . *supportive*.

Trevor couldn't bring himself to look at her while he said the words, so he kept his eyes focused on his knee-caps. "Naw, Corey is a great choice. Perfect, really. He's an eighth grader, and older than me . . . and cooler than me . . . and I'm in the process of becoming great friends with the guy. Seriously . . . probably in the process. No, Lib, it's a great choice."

"Cool," she said, knowing she couldn't tell him what she really thought of Molly.

"Yeah. Cool," Trevor replied, knowing he couldn't tell her what he really thought of Corey.

So Libby turned and looked out the window while

Trevor pressed his head against the back of the seat. And for the rest of the ride home, they didn't say another word.

Trevor Jones

Walking down his
street, alone

3:40 p.m.

"Corey is a great choice!" Did I really say that to her?! The guy is trying to mangle me and now he's going to take my best friend to the dance?

I should tell her the truth. That he's no regular evil eighth grader. Not even double evil . . . he's Big Mac evil. She can't go with that guy. She just can't.

So, yeah, I'm sure at the right time, in the right way, with the right lighting and room temperature, she'll listen to the truth.

I'll bring her snacks. Ranch dip always puts her in a good mood.

WESTSIDE
MIDDLE SCHOOL

TWO DAYS
LATER

Trevor Jones

At the end of his
driveway, hands
tucked deep in
pockets

7:52 a.m.

Naw, come on—I wouldn't call them "excuses." I'm just saying the temperature has been scorching. And the fluorescent lighting at this school? Horrible for telling someone bad news.

I'll talk to her about Corey. Today.

CHAPTER SEVENTEEN

TREVOR DIDN'T TALK TO LIBBY ABOUT COREY. HE KEPT waiting for some sort of sign other than the perfect room temperature in order to spring it on her.

But that temperature never came and neither did their talk. Trevor decided having a discussion that might make someone get enraged and *not* end up with her stomping off and calling his mother would take lots of charisma.

So instead he focused on hope. Hoping she'd see on her own that Corey was an Olympic gold medal-winning jerk. Hoping she'd simply find someone else to go with. Hoping he wouldn't end up looking like the jerk rather than Corey.

He had a lot more hope than he had charisma, so that was that.

Meanwhile, he had to get serious about finding a new

friend. And he also had to figure out a way to talk to Molly again, using actual words. Which he wasn't sure he could do, but it was important since he had to know what time to meet at the dance and what to wear and whether she'd ever give his '73 Johnny Bench back. Luckily, Marty took him to the side and gave him another "lesson" in his "office."

Which meant more note passing techniques explained in the boys' bathroom.

Marty paced the linoleum floor. "Okay, so this time write her a note and use the Tissue Box Method."

"A tissue box? Really? Why can't I just slide the note across her desk?"

"This is middle school. You must be inconspicuous!"

"But does it always have to be sneeze-related?"

Marty ignored his question. There wasn't much time with only five minutes allowed between classes to go to the bathroom, which to Marty seemed like child abuse. Some things in life took *time*. So he had trained himself like he had his Labrador retriever (finest hunting dog around, according to Marty) to only use the bathroom at certain times of the day (a.k.a. before and after school). That way, he could use those five minutes for more meaningful situations. Like note-passing training.

Marty told Trevor to open his notebook and diagram his

foolproof plan. "First, get her attention so she knows what you're doing. Then fake a quick sneeze, or a series of sneezes for authenticity, and grab a tissue. While you blow, place the note in the box, on top of the next tissue. Molly fake sneezes too, follows behind you, and snatches the note from the box while grabbing the next tissue. Done. Not even the actors on *CSI: Miami* would see that one coming."

Trevor had paid very close attention to his instructions. There was no way he was going to get it wrong this time. So the following day in homeroom, Trevor tapped Molly's shoulder, let out a triple fake sneeze, sauntered up to the tissue box, and placed the note inside as he blew his nose.

What he didn't count on was Jake Jacobs's severe ragweed allergy. With unfortunate timing, Jake ripped out an *authentic* triple sneeze and rushed the tissue box. Trevor tried to block his hand before he reached out for it, but Jake was in extreme need of a tissue, otherwise he'd face a colossal nose-drip situation. He shoved Trevor's hand out of the way and snatched a tissue. But he not only snatched a tissue—he snatched the note as well.

While blowing his nose with one hand, Jake opened the note with the other. He flicked his eyes up to Trevor. They stared at each other for an uncomfortable moment— neither one sure what to do next.

But Jake never did find it funny that Trevor had called him a girl on the first day of school. This was his chance to show him middle school was *no place* for making mistakes.

Jake glanced over at Molly then back to Trevor. "I'll give it to her, dude."

Trevor nodded, not sure what to do. And not sure why Jake was being helpful. Maybe Jake realized that Trevor mistaking him for a girl on the first day was just that: a mistake. And everyone's allowed one or two or a dozen of those, right? "Thanks," Trevor said.

Jake swaggered over to Molly, his Vans skater shoes squeaking on the linoleum. Only he didn't stop at Molly's desk. He kept on swaggering. And kept on. All the way until he was across the room and standing next to one Nancy Polanski. Nancy gladly took the note from him.

She read it—twice—then twisted around to get a better view of Trevor as he still stood at the front of the room.

She smiled. Trevor sneezed—a *real* one—and it appeared he was becoming allergic to his own public humiliation.

Trevor sauntered back over to his desk and slumped into his seat. He looked over at Molly, who was busy making a new pattern out of safety pins on her already tattered backpack. She hadn't even seen any of the fake sneeze note-passing catastrophe that just went down. *Why do I even try?* Trevor asked himself.

But relief filled him when he saw Nancy ask Mr. Everett for a bathroom pass and head out of the class and down the hall. She was gone.

Whew. Don't have to worry about her, for a minute at least.

"Trevor." Mr. Everett was now standing at his desk. "You need to get checked out by the nurse." He slid a hall pass across his desk to him.

"I . . . what?"

"All that sneezing. I can't have you getting other students sick."

"But Jake—" Trevor pointed over to him, but Jake held up his bottle of Allegra.

"Allergies," Mr. Everett explained. "He has his medicine. But you need to head on down to the nurse."

The thought of Nancy and her hall pass immediately filled his head. "When you say *down*, do you mean go down the *hall*?"

Mr. Everett raised a brow. "There's no water slide here. You'll have to use the hall."

Trevor slowly walked out of homeroom. He hung his head as he rounded the corner, to see an empty, eerie hallway. Other than the clomping sound of his own shoes echoing off the walls, all he could hear were quiet rumbles from students inside closed classroom doors.

He successfully made it around another corner without running into Nancy, and he saw the gleaming lights of the nurse's office ahead. As he got close, he fake-sneezed one more time in hopes of the nurse keeping him in there for the rest of homeroom, or better yet, the rest of the day. The embarrassment was too much. And a note like that was no doubt going to end up with a massive Nancy Polanski punch to the stomach.

But unfortunately, standing in the nurse's office was Nancy, taking her midmorning vitamin D supplement, which she took three times daily with water; her mother was concerned that she wasn't getting enough vitamin D from the sun since she spent so much time in the gym. Nancy was wearing her velour competitive gymnastics sweat suit—the maroon one, her favorite—which Trevor was concerned gave her superhuman strength.

As they passed each other at the door, Nancy not surprisingly gave him a quick jab to the midsection. She looked amused. "I figured you'd like that." Because Nancy thought that deep down—even though they would never admit it—all boys liked being punched by cute, athletic girls. "See you at the dance. Six p.m. sharp, right?"

Trevor clutched his stomach and silently cursed the person who started the myth that guys *liked* being punched by unusually strong girls, much less *any* girl.

But he decided he *had* to tell her the truth; he couldn't have her giving him stomach punches for the wrong reasons. "That note wasn't for you."

Her face turned the color of her sweat suit. "But why did you have Jake give it to me?"

"He did it as a joke, to get back at me. I . . . I've been trying to make new friends . . . but it's not exactly working out."

She shook her head, then made sure the nurse's back was turned. Then, slugged him in the stomach, yet again.

He bent over, clutching his stomach. "What was *that* for?"

"That's what I do to jerks."

Trevor couldn't believe she had the same move for guys she liked *and* guys she didn't like. But it seemed to make her feel better, and he watched as she trotted happily down the hall, her ponytail swinging back and forth as she headed back to class.

He'd never seen a ponytail have so much pride.

Trevor Jones

Nurse's station,
ice to the stomach

10:20 a.m.

This is getting ridiculous.

Libby made it perfectly clear I could get through this middle school thing if I just scuffed my shoes and didn't talk about my baseball cards.

Maybe my shoes need more scuffing. Is that what my problem is?

CHAPTER EIGHTEEN

AFTER SCUFFING HIS SHOES EVEN MORE WITHOUT noticing much change in his social life, Trevor decided this making new friends stuff was a great hobby for *other* people. No matter what he did, it seemed his attempt to be friendly resulted in either him splattered on the floor or with a punch to the stomach.

So instead he spent lunchtime listening to the Baker twins argue.

And he spent his hallway time discussing survival techniques with Marty.

And Trevor spent Friday afternoons helping Wilson buff the floors clean. Or at least he *hoped* to. Trevor hadn't been formally invited by Wilson to use the floor buffer, but he was pretty determined to make that happen. He was hoping the power of positive thinking would make that dream a reality.

But he did *not* spend his time letting Libby know what he thought of Corey. Not exactly exemplary best friend behavior. So all in all he wasn't getting through this whole middle school thing with much success, but he had a busy life. What did he need friends for?

All he had to do was stay away from Corey Long's evil smirk and tripping foot, and he'd be fine. He had successfully avoided Corey for several days, except he was forced to go out of his way to do so.

But then his luck ran out. As Trevor was leaving homeroom, he looked down the hall and saw Corey drumming on his friend's notebook, impressing a group of girls surrounding him with his rhythm. But he was also standing right in the path of Trevor's next class. There was no way around him.

As he approached, their eyes locked and Trevor froze. He knew that look; there was no way he was going to get by Corey without somehow getting splattered and putting up yet another yard sale on the hallway floor. He was trapped. So he wished for some help, a tornado perhaps.

But what he got was Molly. As she followed behind Trevor, she saw the situation unfold and knew exactly why

Trevor was frozen in the middle of the hall. She'd seen this before.

Having attended three schools in the past year, she had seen all different types of kids, but one thing was the same at every school: there was *always* a Corey Long. The kid who would snow all the teachers and the clueless girls, then torment all the guys and get away with it.

"Stick close to me," Molly said in Trevor's ear. She knew he'd be safe next to her because the one thing Corey couldn't stand most in the world—even more than hair that wouldn't fall into place—was to *not* be adored by a girl. And Corey knew Molly didn't like him one bit. So whenever Molly was around, Corey Long disappeared.

Molly gently led Trevor by the elbow and whispered, "As we walk past Corey, don't leave my side."

Trevor couldn't believe he was about to walk by Corey right there in a hallway—prime tripping real estate. But that thought was overpowered by another one: Molly's hand was on his elbow.

Trevor Jones

In the hallway,
fidgety

11:22 a.m.

Did you see that? She wanted me to be RIGHT next to her while we walked past Corey. She's trying to make him jealous. With me.

So not only are we going to the dance together, but I think she ACTUALLY likes me. Maybe this dance thing is going to turn out to be a good thing after all.

I have GOT to find out what the dress code is.

Sure enough, as Molly and Trevor got closer to Corey, he suddenly stuffed his drumsticks in his back pocket and disappeared into the crowd.

From that day forward, whenever Trevor would find himself being eyeballed by Corey in the hall or in the cafeteria or during one of Wilson's emergency assemblies, Molly would appear and Corey would vanish. It was as if Corey was Superman and Molly was his Kryptonite.

Trevor didn't know why it was working, but all that mattered to him was the fact that Corey wasn't bothering him anymore and Molly was sometimes touching his elbow.

Smooth sailing, Trevor thought.

But his good fortune was short-lived. When Libby was named head of the dance party planning committee, his sailboat suddenly sank.

Cindy Applegate

At her locker,
obsessively
reorganizing
tubes of lip
gloss on the shelf

1:48 p.m.

This is a complete travesty. A total corruption of justice. I'm not going to lie to you—even gum doesn't taste good after hearing this news. WHY won't these tubes of lip gloss STAND UP?!

No, that's not the news. Here's the thing . . . Libby was named head of the dance planning committee. That's right . . . not ME . . . LIBBY. I was BORN for that position. No one but me has a VIP frequent buyer discount card at Parties Plus—they don't just give those out to anyone. You have to buy themed napkins by the CASELOAD to get one.

I mean, I respect Libby's attention to detail and how she balanced the budget when she was sixth grade treasurer and my car wash fund-raiser idea turned into a bit of a disaster. That bottle did NOT say "bubble bath" on it—I swear it just said "soap."

But no one could deny how cute the mayor's SUV looked with all those pink bubbles on it. And, okay, it was cool and all for Libby to take the blame for it and do that community service for the mayor. But I didn't think it was that big of a deal in the first place. I mean who doesn't like cute pink bubbles on cars?

Anyway, Libby had BETTER like cute. Because I am NOT going to a dance decorated with an earthworm theme or whatever she's into. She's probably not even planning on providing gum.

Like I said, complete travesty.

Libby Gardner

At her locker,
obsessively
reorganizing
books on the
shelf

1:55 p.m.

She said I'm going to make the dance an earthworm theme?!

Hey, at least I move my fingers out of the way when I'm reading the label on a bottle of Tropic Pink Flamingo Foaming Bubble Bath. I had to repaint the town's park benches because of her. I mean, those benches really DID need a fresh coat of paint, so it's not like I minded, but still.

No, this dance is going to be awesome. I'm letting loose this time—no earth tones, just all festive colors. This will be the most amazing dance, and my coolest project ever. And if it makes me a shoo-in for seventh grade student council president? Then . . . hey. Two birds, one stone.

·It's just good time management, that's all.

CHAPTER NINETEEN

A COUPLE OF DAYS BEFORE THE DANCE, THE PARTY planning committee met after school in the gym. The floor was full of party supplies and Libby had a list of assignments—a very *long* list—tacked to the wall. Trevor was busy separating the spoons from the forks, but he watched as Libby bounded around the room making sure everyone was doing their job to perfection.

"You're definitely excited about this dance," Trevor said to her as she bounded by.

Libby paused and gazed off, looking down the hall through the glass window of the door. "I just want everything to be . . . perfect."

Trevor followed her line of sight. She was looking at Corey. He wasn't helping with party details; he was, of course, *not* in the gym, but rather down the hall—leaning, slouching, reeking, aligning hairs.

But Trevor looked up and suddenly realized . . . with the fluorescent lights turned off and the afternoon sun streaming in . . . the *lighting* . . . it was perfect for sharing bad news!

"Libby, I have to talk to you about Corey."

"Hand me that streamer," she said.

"Which one? Dark orange or burnt orange?"

"Burnt orange."

"I thought you were going to do fun colors." Trevor scrunched his face. He knew other girls—regular ones— liked things like pink and purple and fun. "These are earth colors," he explained.

She shook her head. "No. It's *festive.* It's orange."

"It's the color of most of Utah."

She sighed and stuck her hand on her hip. "Just tell me what you wanted to say about Corey."

"It's about that day . . ."

"Which day, Trev? There are lots of them."

"The first day of school—when he told you he helped me out? He didn't."

She planted her *other* hand on her *other* hip.

Trevor knew that wasn't a good sign. He gripped the

Utah orange streamer in his hand. "He *tricked* me into going in the teachers' bathroom and then he *tripped* me when I came out."

"He wouldn't do that on purpose."

"Purpose. It was on!" Trevor was nervous—back to Yoda-speak.

"Trevor, people get directions in this school wrong all the time. I still don't know how to find the office. And maybe you tripped over his feet. That isn't uncommon."

Before Trevor could explain, Libby had turned the focus back to party planning detail. "Now, hand me those balloons, and we need to clean these floors and work on improving the lighting." She clapped her hands and marched off. "Mood lighting, people! The dance is only fifty hours and thirty-three minutes away!"

Trevor turned away, stunned that she wouldn't even consider his side of the story. He tried to get his mind on sturdy plastic silverware, but Libby sauntered back over to him to get in one last thing. "Seriously, Corey's a good guy," she said in a whispering instructional tone. "He calls me all the time and we work together on our math homework. This is totally turning into something. Don't ruin this for me. I wouldn't say anything bad about Molly. I wouldn't dare say that she's trouble and likes to take things from

197

people and clearly enjoys getting detention. I'd never do that to you. So be my friend, Trevor, and get some plastic forks from Wilson's Supply Containment Unit."

Trevor rolled his eyes. "You mean the janitor's *closet*?"

"Don't be rude."

He lowered his head and scuffled out to the ~~closet~~ unit where supplies were contained, which was in the hallway—the same hallway where Corey Long was busy being evil. Uh, not good. Trevor thought about showing Libby firsthand what type of a guy Corey really was. Corey was using a black Sharpie to vandalize words on the dance poster hanging in the hall.

But Libby was busy, happily refolding all the napkins Cindy had just folded. Trevor couldn't bear to bring her down when she was *that* happy.

But he still had to get in that closet. Trevor looked in all directions, but Molly was nowhere to be found. It didn't make sense to him. Libby had delegated party planning jobs out to everyone in homeroom. So why wasn't Molly there? Shouldn't she be helping out with mood lighting and being Kryptonite to Corey?

"She's late. That's all," Trevor told himself. "She'll show. She always does."

Molly

About to head into an afternoon detention, slight smile

3:05 p.m.

I do NOT do party planning.

No. Way.

Detention is waaaaay more interesting for an after-school activity. Plus, I heard a rumor from Cindy Applegate that the theme is carrots and earthworms or something. I don't trust her sources for one second, but if that's even partially true, I am going to have to find a way to make this dance REMOTELY entertaining.

After a few minutes of waiting for Molly's sudden well-timed appearance, Trevor gave up and realized he'd have to get to that closet on his own.

The moment Trevor saw Corey distracted by a flyaway hair strand, he tiptoed softly down the hall, Christmas present–hunting style, and quietly slipped inside the closet.

Whew, Trevor thought. I did it. And *without* Molly. That wasn't so hard!

Trevor leaned against the storage shelves to keep hidden from view, being careful not to disturb any items as they appeared to be meticulously organized. Wow. Libby should see this, he thought, admiring Wilson's commitment to order. But then he heard Corey and his sidekicks talking. Trevor peeked through the crack in the door and saw Corey and his crew walking toward the closet. When they were only a few feet away, Trevor could hear their conversation very clearly.

"Look at all those lame decorations," Corey said, as he peered through the window of the door to the gym, where Libby was organizing her team of frenzied decorating elves.

One of his sidekicks chimed in. "And I heard they're going to have raw vegetables for a snack. Did you hear me? Raw, dude. This girl has to be stopped."

Spaz, his other sidekick, chimed in too. "Why are you even going with that girl?"

"I *had* to ask her. Nicole is the only one I know who actually understands that algebra stuff. She's been doing all my homework for me."

"She fell for the nice handwriting line?" Spaz asked.

"She fell hard. Might even get some history report writing out of her. I just have to take her to this dance and I'm guaranteed a decent grade."

"Sure, but *raw*? Seriously?"

"I'll fix this. She'll do whatever I ask. Don't worry."

Trevor clenched his fist. He's using her for *grades*? He can't remember her *name*?

Corey and his goons started walking, but as they passed the door, Trevor saw Corey's evil foot—a foot he would recognize anywhere—as it kicked the door shut.

Click.

Trevor jiggled the handle. He jiggled it again, and again. Nothing! He was locked inside—completely trapped! Minutes went by. Quite a few of them. He wasn't sure how to escape and the only thing he had with him was his lucky pen.

No one was coming to free him, and Trevor wasn't about to scream for Corey to save him. I'll spend the night on this cement floor before I'll get help from that meathead, he thought.

In actuality, Trevor wasn't much of a naturalist, and he'd rather spend the night in his own bed than sleep in the wild. His comforter was half down feather, half moose fur; he valued extreme comfort. So he waited until he could no longer hear Corey and his sidekicks, then searched for a way to get out.

He felt around until he found the light switch and flipped it on.

There was a floor buffer. Window cleaner. Napkins. Plastic forks. An emergency satellite cell phone.

How am I going to get out of here?

And then he spotted it—exactly what he needed to escape.

A spray can of Easy Cheese.

Wilson

Straightening supplies in his Containment Unit

4:15 p.m.

Yes sirree, I was the one who found Trevor in the Containment Unit. He was lucky too, because everyone else had gone home—including Vice Principal Decker, who would not have been happy about a rogue student eating his way through the snacks in the Unit.

So apparently Trevor found my secret stash—the Easy Cheese . . . it's the only thing that gets me through the Friday afternoon floor buffings. But squeezing Easy Cheese under the door to spell "Help" was not a good idea. Someone could've slipped. The cell phone probably would've been the better choice. Less mess.

But no, I'm not gonna give that kid detention. I have much better plans for him.

Trevor Jones

Cleaning the floor
inside Wilson's
Containment Unit
4:17 p.m.

Libby is going to FREAK when I tell her why Corey really asked her to the dance.

Well, sure I'm going to TELL her. I have to, right?

I mean, she didn't believe that he tripped me, but she's SURE to believe this.

Except I'm not sure when to talk to her. Tomorrow Wilson has me buffing floors. Which is pretty much a dream come true. Have you ever used a floor buffer?

It's like watching a double feature of *Alien Star Invaders 2: The Invasion* followed by *Body Invasion 3: The Alien Relocation*. . . .

Awesome!!!

WESTSIDE
MIDDLE SCHOOL

THE NEXT
DAY

Trevor Jones

Standing outside
homeroom, peeking in

8:20 a.m.

Today is the day. And I've heard morning is a great time to break bad news. I have to tell her the truth.

WESTSIDE
MIDDLE SCHOOL

MINUTES
LATEЯ

Trevor Jones

Still outside
homeroom

8:29 a.m.

I can't tell her the truth.

Except the dance is tomorrow. If I tell her, there is no way she'll have enough time to get a different date.

But if I don't tell her, she might think Corey really likes her and get her feelings hurt. She's been trying to impress him—the girl's worn a skirt every day this week. That can't be a coincidence.

Aw, man.

Every time I have a problem, it's Libby who tells me what to do. So how do I figure out a problem about HER?

I can't believe I'm saying this, but . . . I'm going to have to rely on my own instincts. I really don't see any other choice here.

CHAPTER TWENTY

AFTER CONSULTING HIS MAGIC 8 BALL, HIS HOROSCOPE, and a mood ring without much help, Trevor finally flipped a coin and had to approach Libby at her locker. After all, tails are tails.

He tapped her shoulder. "So that thing I wanted to tell you about Corey?"

She perked up and turned around. "Yeah?" Her eyebrows were arched, not scrunched, which Trevor thought was a good sign.

But even though Trevor enjoyed looking at her encouraging arched eyebrows, he knew it was time. "On the first day, when he sent me into the teachers' bathroom and then he tripped me when I came running out? He's been reminding me of it ever since. Every day, there it is. That foot. Taunting me."

Encouraging!

Not encouraging. In fact, do I owe this girl money?

"Trevor, why are you bringing this up again? He wouldn't do that to you." Libby couldn't believe he was saying this. Corey was not mean. In fact, he'd been *so* sweet to her. They'd been doing their homework together and Corey even told her that she had the best handwriting of any girl he'd ever done his homework with before. And he let her write the answers to the problems on his paper because her handwriting was *that* good. He even offered to start doing history homework together. You simply can't find a nicer guy than Corey Long, Libby thought.

"The guy is *totally* evil, Libby!" Trevor threw his arms in the air. "How could you like a guy like that?"

"Why are you doing this?" She reached into her backpack and pulled out a small container.

"You keep emergency ranch dip in your backpack?"

She dipped her finger in and took a taste. "Where else am I going to keep it?!"

She turned from him and started walking away, but he galloped alongside her, doing his best to keep up. "I'm just trying to help. Because he . . ." Oh, man, here goes nothing, he thought. "He didn't ask you to the dance because he likes you."

"What?" She stopped in her tracks. "Why *else* would he ask me?"

"I know the real reason." He swallowed hard, wondering if he should keep going. He didn't want to hurt her feelings, but she *had* to know. He figured that was what apologies were for. "Corey only asked you so you'd do his algebra work for him. I overheard him say it. He's not the sharpest variable in the equation, if you know what I mean."

"You heard wrong. It's not true. We hang out all the time."

"And do *homework*?"

She looked away. "Don't talk to me anymore, Trevor."

"Come on, Libby. Don't be mad."

"I'm mad," Libby said as she marched off because she wasn't going to listen to Trevor make up horrible lies about Corey.

Trevor almost ran after her to apologize, but he stood frozen in the hall. He realized *she* wasn't the one who should be mad, *he* should be. After all, he was the one who'd been her best friend since they potty trained, not Corey. Why wouldn't she believe him? Wasn't that her job?

Trevor called after her, "You can't be mad at me. I'm mad at *you*!"

Libby answered, but she kept walking. "I'm still mad!"

Trevor dropped his head and whispered, "I'm telling my mom."

"Still mad," Libby said under her breath as she disappeared around the corner.

CHAPTER TWENTY-ONE

LIBBY FIGURED SHE SHOULD CALL **T**REVOR'S MOTHER. She always told Ms. Jones whatever was going on with Trevor—detail by painful detail—and Libby had never been mad at Trevor for longer than an eleven-minute cartoon episode, so this event undoubtedly warranted a phone conversation with his mom.

But Libby wasn't mad. She was devastated. Why would Trevor lie to her? All those times she stood up for him, and he repaid her with a horrible lie? As much as Libby wanted to call Ms. Jones and tell her every aching detail of the type of person her son had turned into, she simply couldn't do it. Libby knew Ms. Jones was a big contributor to the Girl Power Fund of America (helping girls realize they *rock* since 1992!), so if Ms. Jones found out Trevor had hurt a girl's feelings, she would no doubt hang him by his toes and stop feeding him. Or at least take away the good snacks.

As much as Libby wanted to get back at him, she didn't want Trevor to have to spend the rest of his life upside down—hungry. So she kept it to herself.

Trevor bolted through the front door. "Mom, if the phone rings, don't answer it."

Ms. Jones was cheerfully pulling groceries out of a bag. "Problem at school?"

"No. Just a problem with . . ." He didn't know how to say this. A problem with Libby, the kind where he'd hurt her feelings? Even if she was the one who'd made him mad, he couldn't admit to his mom he'd upset a girl; he'd never eat again.

"I think I know what this is about." She pulled a stool out from the kitchen counter and motioned for him to sit. "You need to tell someone the truth. And it's eating away at you, but you know the longer you wait the worse it gets."

Wow. Do moms know everything? Trevor wondered. "How do you know everything?"

"Voice mail." She held up a *How to Draw Cartoon Figures* book. "The library left a message today. Trevor, I appreciate your passion for drawing, but you have to return your books on time. And if they're overdue, just tell me."

Trevor was shocked by his overdue library book, but it was a clear indication that all this stuff going on at school was distracting him. There had to be a way to handle this problem without accumulating late fees.

And since moms seemed to know everything, she was the one he needed to get help from—no matter the consequences.

"It's not a library problem, Mom . . . it's a girl problem. I think I hurt a girl's feelings, but I was trying to protect her. Except now *I'm* the bad guy, and I don't know how to fix this."

Ever since the divorce, Ms. Jones wondered when she'd have to give Trevor the "girl talk." The one she had rehearsed over and over and would give in a brief, two-sentence format. She cleared her throat and said, "With girls, you can't do much with their feelings other than this: let them have them. We girls have feelings *all* the time, and we like it that way."

This didn't make sense to Trevor. It was like girls were another species. "Let me see if I have this right. You mean she'd rather know the truth so she can have her own feelings about the truth, even if those feelings about the truth make her feel bad because they're *her* feelings and she just likes having them?"

Ms. Jones winked at him. "That's my boy."

"But I told her the truth, and she got mad. I don't know what I did wrong."

"It's not about *how* you tell her, it's *why* you tell her. That's what will make you the good guy."

Except Trevor wasn't sure why he told her. So she wouldn't get hurt by Corey later? So she'd go to the dance with someone else? Did it matter *why* he told her? There were too many questions that he figured he'd never know the answer to. He pushed away from the counter and said, "I don't know . . . this being a good guy thing is too hard to figure out."

Ms. Jones couldn't stand seeing the sad look on his face. "It's my fault. I've been putting too much pressure on you since the divorce." She straightened his collar. "But can you blame me for trying to make you into the perfect young man? Your future wife and president of America will thank me someday!" She winked.

Trevor's eyes grew big, like Frisbees. He valued being prepared, but this was a little *too* much planning ahead. "I'm twelve, Mom. I'm not getting married anytime this week. So can you just help me figure out my Libby problem?"

Ms. Jones stepped back, startled. She thought this was a *girl* problem, not a Libby problem. She tilted her head, looking very confused.

Trevor realized that if he was going to get help from the person who knew *everything*, he was going to have to tell her *everything*. Or close to it. He took a deep breath and blurted it out. "Libby got asked to the dance by Corey Long, but he's a professional jerk—details I don't want to get into—but she hasn't seen him being a jerk and she thinks I'm lying about all of this for reasons I do not know. Is it hot in here?"

"Does she like him?"

He slumped his shoulders. "She's worn a skirt every day this week."

"Let her keep her feelings, Trevor. She can decide for herself. That's how you can be a friend to her." Ms. Jones tapped him on the nose. "And when in doubt, apologize." She said it like this was all so easy to figure out. He couldn't help but wonder when things would be easy for *him* to figure out.

Ms. Jones's phone rang.

Trevor reached out. "Don't answer—"

"Hello? Really? He did? No, Trevor didn't tell me that. Of course I'll volunteer. Thank you!"

Trevor braced for impact—what had he not told her? Surely it wasn't another late library book.

"It was your teacher, Mr. Everett. Apparently you've had several slipping incidents so far this year?"

Trevor hung his head, wishing he *had* gone into the details of Corey's evilness—it would explain all this mess.

But his mom was already busy filling in her calendar. "They want me to volunteer at the dance as a chaperone. They're worried you may slip again and they feel you need extra supervision. You're a liability on the school's insurance policy." She looked down at his feet. "It's those shoes. They're too worn and scuffed. Plus it must be embarrassing for you to have such filthy shoes. I'll get some of those new kind with the thick soles. They improve your posture, too. I read an article in a magazine once that said bad posture is the cause of the majority of locker jammings. Written by an actual janitor too."

"Mom, I don't want new shoes."

"And you'll need a crisp, white shirt for the dance. Maybe some pleated khakis. Don't want you to go looking like you just came from school. Believe me . . . I remember these things from when I was a kid. A dance is a *dance*— not school. And Trevor, I'll get to see the *whole* thing. I can't wait to meet your date! What's her name?"

He was hoping to never have this conversation, but he was the one who'd brought it up. He couldn't stop talking now; she'd never let him. "Her name is Molly."

She raised an eyebrow. "And she was in Honor Society with you?"

"She's new."

"New," Ms. Jones repeated. She tilted her head and flicked her eyes up, clearly poised for more information, and Trevor knew this meant she wanted details.

"She . . . she likes baseball," he added.

"Baseball. An athletic girl. I like that," Ms. Jones said with lots of perk.

Trevor knew his mom might not have the right impression of Molly, but maybe since it was a dance, there'd be a dress code and she'd show up in something crisp and clean.

But then again, the last thing Mysterious Molly ever seemed to do was follow the rules.

Cindy Applegate

School parking lot,
applying lip gloss

Saturday, 5:45 p.m.

So the dance is tonight. And I'm not nervous at all or anything, but I am wondering if going with Marty was the best choice.

No, I mean . . . that's true—I didn't technically HAVE another choice. But still. I just like making highly informed decisions. All I know about the guy is that he shoots things. For sport or something? I hope he doesn't hand over a dead deer to my father—a gesture, I think they call it. Which would be wicked gross. No, all he has to do is replenish my supply of Hubba Bubba Strawberry Watermelon gum. I am a totally simple girl.

Okay, so—not that I'm obsessing or anything—but you know that ranch dip? I finally convinced Libby fat-free was the way to go. She was really busy hanging up streamers—those Grand Canyon colored ones—but I'm pretty sure she said okay.

Or maybe she said, "No way."

Nah. I'm sure she's fine with it. I mean, it

tastes just the same! There is no need for extra caloric intake when taste isn't compromised. That's my motto.

My other motto is: Never leave the house without a backup pack of gum, or at least a guy who will provide the backup gum.

You can use that if you want.

CHAPTER TWENTY-TWO

TREVOR AND LIBBY HADN'T SPOKEN SINCE THEIR argument. It was the night of the dance and Trevor arrived not just on time, but early—first, because his mother was now one of the chaperones and had to get there early for a chaperone briefing meeting Decker was giving in his office. Apparently he was giving a lesson on how to spot inappropriate dance moves—there would be a PowerPoint presentation and everything.

But Trevor also arrived early because Molly asked him to. That was because Molly, despite her efforts to avoid *all* party planning duties, had to take the job of making sure the chairs were lined up against the gym wall before the dance started. That only occurred because Mr. Everett stepped in and warned Molly she *had* to perform a duty, otherwise he would have her spend the afternoon decorating his class bulletin boards. Molly thought putting things on a bulletin board would be fantastic, given her artistic ability at poking things with safety pins—she had *big* plans. But Mr. Everett signed her name next to chair duty and changed the consequence to chalkboard washing, so Molly gave in and decided to show up for the chair arranging.

When his mom and the other chaperones disappeared around the corner, headed to Decker's chaperone preparedness training, Trevor stood in the hall, not quite sure what to do. Suddenly, Molly walked up behind him and poked him in the back. "Hey," she said in an already-bored voice.

He twirled around. "Need help with the chairs?" Trevor asked as he nervously tucked and un-tucked his brand-new shirt, unsure of middle school dance dress code. Dressy? Relaxed? Dressy relaxed? Who really knew? Was it written somewhere?

DANCE ENTRY TICKET

Welcome to the 7th/8th grade dance!
Where 7th and 8th graders will dance in the same room!

TIME: Doors open at 6 p.m. sharp!
ALSO: Healthy snacks are provided.
ALSO: No sugar allowed within 50 feet of loud music, strictly enforced with detention slips.
ATTIRE: Normal school clothes, relaxed, NOT DRESSY!

Molly *had* read her ticket. She wore the exact same thing she had worn to school—a jean miniskirt with ripped black tights and a green army jacket, held together with safety pins that gave off a clanging sound that made Trevor strangely comfortable. "No, I don't need help with the chairs," she said as she glanced up and down the empty hallway. "But the decorations are supposed to be a surprise, so I need you to stand by the door. Libby said no one goes in the gym before six. So this is the important part: do not let *anyone* in."

Trevor wasn't sure what to say. True, she was being rather pushy. And her request was pretty strange. But given the fact that Libby wasn't speaking to him at all, he simply appreciated the direct communication—no matter how strange and pushy.

"I can do that." Trevor felt good. Like he was helping out in some way and he thought maybe—just *maybe*—Libby would appreciate his help. And possibly even speak to him again. And that would be cool.

Trevor stood with his arms crossed as people started to line up outside the doors. "Can't go in until six."

As the crowd grew bigger, waiting to get in there, they grew rowdy. They even started chanting, "Let us in! Let us in!" As if their personal partying rights had been stripped.

Trevor worried this was getting seriously close to showing up on CNN.

Libby rushed through the front door, going over her mental checklist of final party preparations. She looked around for Corey, but didn't see him, so she headed inside by herself, lugging in one final party decoration: an inflatable saguaro cactus. A *very festive* inflatable saguaro cactus.

She saw a group had formed outside the gym doors, and she pushed through the anxious (but also surprisingly calm because really . . . it's not cool to look *that* anxious) mob and marched up to Trevor with her cactus in hand, unknowingly whacking people from behind as she made her way. "What are you doing? Open the doors!"

"Molly said you told her not to let them in until six. I'm being helpful. Right?" Trevor smiled, enjoying the fact that they were having something similar to a conversation.

"I never told her that. Molly is in charge of *chairs*. That's it. And they were supposed to be done *last night*."

Trevor suddenly realized Molly had neglected her job. And that was why they were there early—for Molly to do the duty she was supposed to have already finished.

Since he and Libby hadn't spoken since their fight, he figured a desperate situation like this could definitely lead to a conversation. "I'll open the doors if . . . if you'll come talk to me." He hoped to pull Libby away in time so she wouldn't see that Molly hadn't done her job. As much as he was perplexed by Molly's lack of responsible behavior, he didn't want her to end up on Libby's Icky List. It wasn't a long list, so there was room on there.

Libby looked at the anxious crowd. "Fine. Fine! Just open the doors!"

He yanked the doors open and saw Molly sneaking out through the back exit. Luckily he didn't have to shield Libby from Molly's laziness . . . the chairs were all placed neatly along the walls and the cafeteria looked perfect. Not a balloon or streamer out of place.

"Wow," Libby whispered to herself. "I'm pretty good at this delegating thing."

Even though Trevor now did not technically have to drag Libby away to talk, he couldn't help but take advantage of the situation. Libby had agreed to talk . . . to *him*. It would be one of those back-and-forth things . . . a *conversation*! Trevor stiffened up and prepared to go into Conversational Apology Mode.

"Come on, Lib." Trevor walked out to a near-empty hallway and Libby followed. "Listen, I'm sorry for what I said about Corey. Maybe he only does evil stuff to me."

She smiled slightly.

"And he probably likes you for more than your algebra answers," Trevor added.

Her slight smile quickly turned into a full-on frown. "I can't believe you're still saying this about Corey. I'm not making up stuff about Molly being some sort of convict or something."

"I'm sorry," he said. "I was just trying to—"

"Have fun tonight Trevor. Without me." She turned and briskly walked down the hall.

Whoa. Wait. Trevor's mom had always taught him that apologies work. Why wasn't this working?

But he couldn't fix this—Libby was already gone.

Trevor scuffled back toward the cafeteria to find Molly. *Surely Libby was kidding about Molly being a convict. Right?*

And that's when he heard the screaming.

Trevor Jones

Outside the
cafeteria,
pacing, extreme

6:02 p.m.

Two minutes into the dance and Libby was screaming. But I couldn't blame her. What I saw when I walked in that room was shocking. The music was cranked, everyone was jumping around, sort of dancing but mostly making weird jerky movements. Hair was flying. But that wasn't the bad part.

There were crumbs and wrappers everywhere.

That's why Libby was screaming.

The chaperones—my MOM included—had spent too much time in training and were late getting back to the gym. Someone had replaced the carrots and spring water with Zingers and orange soda. And not just regular Chocolate Zingers—they were assorted flavors. I even spotted a raspberry one!

But that's not important right now.

Everyone was heavily amped up on sugar, which, of course, led to massive party decoration destruction. They popped balloons. Rearranged chairs. Ripped down Utah-colored streamers.

It was total chaos.

And knowing Libby, she would blame herself.

CHAPTER TWENTY-THREE

BEFORE TREVOR COULD FIND LIBBY OR MOLLY, HIS mother suddenly appeared by his side. "I can't believe someone ruined your dance. What a disaster. I'm just glad MY son, or anyone he knows, would never do something like this." She looked him over. "You don't know who did this, right?"

"Of course not!"

"Good, because you know how I have feelings about—"

"Being disappointed. I know. You don't have to worry, Mom."

She grinned and said, "Speaking of *not* disappointing, where is this date of yours? Can I meet her?"

"Uh, I'm not sure where she is actually." Trevor had a feeling his mom wouldn't be as excited about Molly as she'd like to be. Ripped clothes—on purpose—made no sense to Ms. Jones. So Trevor was secretly glad Molly was missing at that particular moment.

"I'd better help get this place back in order," Ms. Jones said. "It was part two of the training . . . what to do in case of all-out breakdown in behavior." Ms. Jones walked off, ordering students to stop wrapping themselves in streamers.

Before Trevor could go find Molly or Libby, he was stopped again when Corey charged up to him. "Where's Nicole? I have to tell her how cool it is she got Zingers and orange soda instead of those carrots."

This was now starting to make sense to Trevor. He was blaming Libby, but it must have been Corey who switched all the snacks—he was just too embarrassed for his friends to see him with a date who brought carrots and a blow-up cactus to a dance. This whole situation was getting complicated. So Trevor thought about his one obvious option: turning around and running away. But he was tired of that option, and he was tired of Libby getting her feelings hurt. Didn't Corey's mom ever have the "girl talk" with him? Did he even know girls *had* feelings, much less *lots* of them?

So instead, Trevor squared his shoulders up and leaned in a little. "Her name isn't Nicole, it's LIBBY. And you don't even like her. You only asked her because you needed help with algebra. Admit it!"

"How do you know that? Were you spying or something?"

He wasn't about to tell Corey he'd gotten locked in the janitor's closet because of him, and with only a can of Easy Cheese for survival. So he shrugged rather calmly. "The gossip flies fast around here, I guess."

Corey held up his paper cup—recently emptied of orange soda—and crumpled it slowly and deliberately for Trevor to watch every bend and fold. He knew Corey was saying *he* was about to be that cup, so he started to reevaluate the benefits of that running away option. Except Vice Principal Decker stormed up to them. "What happened here?!"

"Sir, I was just telling Corey that I think he only asked Libby to the dance because—"

"I mean with the chaos in here. Why is everyone eating junk food and destroying school property?!"

Corey slyly tucked the Raspberry Zinger in his hand into his back pocket.

Smoosh.

Vice Principal Decker didn't notice and narrowed his eyes at Trevor instead. "Who is in charge of the party planning?"

"I am, sir." Libby walked up to them, shoulders slumped.

"Libby, why would you give them these sorts of snacks?" Decker was getting redder with every screech and holler in the background. "You know it's now against the new school policy to administer anything containing high-fructose corn syrup to students when there is music present."

"I—I know. I delegated duties. Other people were responsible for snacks. I don't know who would've done this. But I was in charge, so I take the blame."

Vice Principal Decker turned to Trevor. "Do you know who did this?"

"I—I . . ."

Trevor and Libby exchanged looks. There was sheer terror in her eyes. Trevor knew she had never gotten so much as a stern look from a teacher, so he knew being blamed for the biggest chaotic breakdown ever in student behavior at a school-sponsored function was, to Libby, even ickier than twins.

And if she got a detention, Libby knew exactly what the consequence would be: a blemished permanent record and no chance of being able to run for student council president. Her seventh grade year would be ruined.

Before Trevor answered Vice Principal Decker's question, he eyebrowed to Libby, *I'm sorry.*

Trevor Jones

Peeking inside
the gym

6:20 p.m.

Okay, so you know those scenes in movies where the guy does the right thing and takes the blame or takes the bullet or drinks the poison or whatever and he saves the girl and saves the world and he turns into an amazing hero?

Yeah, so, at that moment? When Vice Principal Decker asked me that question? I didn't do any of those things.

I didn't save the girl. And I could have. The same girl who always covered for me, no matter what. And I didn't do it.

I could've just said, "Yes, I was the one who put Zingers and orange soda on the tables."

How hard would that have been?

So what did I do instead? Told the truth. And not just any truth. Oh no. I told ALL the excessive details of the truth.

I believe they call that Advanced Truth.

And I am dumb.

"Trevor, son, answer my question. Do you know who did this?"

"I was in charge of forks." There was a quiet pause. Trevor took a deep breath, and then he sort of . . . went for it. "But I couldn't even get that right because Corey kicked the door closed and locked me in the janitor's Supply Containment Unit so I used Easy Cheese to write 'Help' under the door, which really upset Wilson for safety reasons, but he didn't give me detention, just floor-buffing duties, so you see all those clean hallway floors? That's all me, but no, I don't know who did it."

Corey and Libby dropped their mouths.

Vice Principal Decker continued with his squint. Then finally, he turned to Libby. "I don't understand anything Trevor just said, so unless I find out otherwise, I'm holding you responsible for this mess. That means you are stripped of your party planning committee status. And it's also a detention." He placed the pink slip in Libby's hand and charged off toward the rowdy students.

Libby pressed her lips together, holding back tears because she was *not* a crier. She stormed off to the bleachers where she flopped down and buried her face in her hands. Even face smothering was better than crying, Libby thought. She reached into her backpack to get the one thing that could make her happy: her Hola! Kitty Cat! sketchpad. But it was missing. Missing?! Luckily she had a cup of ranch dressing stashed in her backpack or else she really *would* have started crying.

Corey checked his hair and pulled on some hair strands to make sure they were hanging long over his eyes but, of course, not directly *in* his eyes, then turned to Trevor and said, "Awesome. I'm going to go talk to her."

"Why?" Trevor squinted at him. Was Corey really going to *console* her?

"Libby got *detention*. How cool is that?!"

"*Now* you know her name? *Now* you like her? Because she got in *trouble*?!"

"Awesome, right? A bad girl."

"No. Not awesome. That's not who she is. She's freakishly organized, she color coordinates, she's in charge of my social life, she's—"

"And now you're starting to annoy me again." He poked Trevor on the chest. Hard. "I'm going to talk to Libby."

Trevor coughed. It was quite a hard poke, apparently. But Trevor also wasn't the toughest kid around.

"No." Trevor took a deep breath and held his chest tight. "You're going to tell her the truth."

Corey turned back. "I'm going to walk over there and

A backbone would help here, or even a chestbone.

tell her how cool it is that she got detention. That's *all* I'm telling her. And if you tell her, I'll say you're lying. And I don't know if you know much about girls, but they hate liars."

"She'd believe me. We're friends."

"And wouldn't a friend have taken the blame for all this?"

Trevor clenched his jaw. "*You* certainly didn't."

"I'm not her friend. I'm her boyfriend. *Big* difference."

Corey laughed and headed over to Libby as she sat on the

bleachers, calming herself down with salad dressing.

Trevor thought about Libby saying they were only friends, not *friend* friends. And as he watched her struggle to hold back tears, all because she had to take the blame for something she didn't do . . . it hit him . . . the double use of the "friend"—he knew what she meant. It wasn't that she wanted *other* friends—she wanted *better* friends. The kind that would stick up for *her*.

As Trevor watched Libby across the room with Corey, her hands flying as she talked away—using more words with Corey than she had used with Trevor the past two weeks—his stomach dropped. He had lost his best and seemingly *only* friend—to a completely evil goon. What could he do about it? He thought it over, then realized that without a locker door around for face-planting, he only had one other option: sit on the floor and lean against the concrete wall in utter and complete defeat.

He slid down the wall and dropped his head.

"Are we going to dance or something?" Molly stood at Trevor's feet. "If not, then let's go." She slung her backpack over her shoulder. "This is sooo boring."

Trevor leaned to the side a little to get a glimpse of the students running around wildly, wrapping themselves in streamers, looking like orange mummies, and evading the chaperones while Vice Principal Decker, who was wielding a large stack of pink detention slips, ran after them.

"This? *This* is boring?"

Molly spun around to watch the group. "It was cool for like a minute."

Trevor noticed her backpack was overly stuffed and not completely zipped up. But something about it seemed off—even for Molly, it appeared to be a little *too* over-stuffed. He hopped up to his feet and peered in. And he couldn't believe what he saw.

Trevor Jones

Hiding behind the
bleachers, nervous
peering

6:45 p.m.

Carrots. Her backpack is stuffed with carrots! SHE'S the one who switched out the snacks. That must be why she wanted to get in the room by herself before the dance started.

Molly is to blame. And she's my date. Maybe I shouldn't be so picky, but ruining the dance and blaming my best friend for it is sort of a dealbreaker for me.

I'm going to have to confront her to clear Libby's name. Otherwise Libby will never be friends with me again if she finds out the truth.

But Molly. Mysterious Molly . . .

She has blue streaks in her hair. She loves rare baseball cards. She's almost perfection. And she's the first girl to ever write the word YES on paper in response to me asking a girl to a dance.

I don't mean to be negative or anything, and you can censor this out if you have to, but I just realized something.

This . . . **CENSORED**

I don't know what to do. Do you have a Magic 8 Ball?

Please. I'm desperate.

Trevor quickly reached into his pocket and pulled out the miniature Magic 8 Ball Molly had traded him for the baseball card. He turned away from her and whispered into the small ball, "Should I tell Vice Principal Decker Molly is to blame?" Then he shook it and looked for his answer to appear in the tiny, tiny window.

There were letters, but they were too small and blurry to read.

He was going to have to fix this without the use of a magic ball. He'd have to do this on his own.

"You're the one who switched the snacks," Trevor said to Molly.

She spun back around to face him and pushed her backpack away from him. "What are you talking about?"

"You have a backpack full of carrots." He looked down at her fidgety hands. "And there's Zinger frosting on your fingers."

She glanced at her hand, then squinted at him as she licked the frosting off. "What's the big deal? No one got hurt."

"Libby did. She got in trouble. You have to tell the vice principal you did it."

"I'm not telling Dad anything."

"Yes, you're going to tell him—wait. What? Did you say *dad*?"

Molly rolled her eyes. "Oh, come on. Why doesn't anyone ever ask me what my last name is? I'm Molly Decker. That man is my dad." She pointed at him as he chased after hyperactive mummies. "And he thinks I'm an angel. He'd never believe you. So let's go. This is now getting seriously boring."

"But . . . why would you do this?"

She huffed, then finally said, "I'll tell you exactly why. Dad comes up with some new strange policy at every school he's assigned to and somebody always challenges it and eventually we get moved." Molly paused and shook her head. "Do you have any idea how boring it gets starting at a new school every few months? How hard it is to start over *all* the time? I *have* to find a way to make my life interesting." She readjusted her backpack on her shoulder. "Don't worry about getting to know me, Trevor—I'll be gone soon anyway. See you around." Molly turned, her safety pins making that clangy sound, and disappeared into the crowd.

Molly Decker

Standing next to
the exit sign,
drinking orange soda

7:01 p.m.

Seriously, every school I go to, it's the same old thing. A crusty old literature teacher, a science teacher who wears Hawaiian shirts and sandals, a janitor who takes his job way too seriously.

And the students? Don't get me started. All the same. They're either jocks or Barbies or metalheads or skaters or gamers or YouTubers. No variation. All the same.

Do you know how boring that gets? All I want is to have interesting things happen. To meet some interesting people. Is that too much to ask? I thought maybe Trevor would be one of those interesting people. Guess I was wrong. He doesn't understand me one bit.

Dad thinks I have a problem—that I have an attention deficit disorder and I need to eat more leafy greens. No. He doesn't get that it's just a straightforward boredom problem.

So yeah, sometimes I make unusual things happen.

A girl's gotta stay awake.

Marty Nelson

At the drink table, calmly pouring a cup of orange soda

7:05 p.m.

Trevor? Oh, man. I was so embarrassed for the guy. He was sitting on the floor mumbling questions at some tiny ball. That wasn't going to solve his problem, whatever it was.

Clearly, the guy had a problem. And I didn't mind being the one to point it out to him.

Yeah, I know there's a rule about seventh and eighth graders being friends. But, hey, I'm the one who made up that rule.

So I can also be the one who breaks it.

CHAPTER TWENTY-FOUR

"**Y**OU'RE SITTING ON THE FLOOR.**" MARTY KICKED** at the bottom of Trevor's shoe. "Come on, get up."

"I'm just going to sit here . . . lean against this wall. . . ."

"You can't lean against a wall all night."

"Going to lean against this wall for eternity, actually. It's a nice wall. A good wall. I call him Wall-y."

"You can't *name* a wall. I won't let you. Get up, Trevor."

"But—"

"Now!"

Trevor looked up at Marty as he peered down on him, looking similar to a forty-story building with a shaved head. Marty was wearing a gray sweatshirt and camouflage pants—the exact same thing he'd worn to school. How does everyone else know dress codes? Trevor wondered.

Trevor took a deep breath, stuffed the Magic 8 Ball in his pocket, and slowly stood up.

Marty crossed his arms. "That thing giving you all the answers?"

"Not a single one."

"What's the problem?"

"I messed everything up. Molly is the one who switched all the snacks, but I didn't know what she was doing and I was the one who stood guard for her while she did it, so technically it's *my* fault that Libby has detention and now Corey likes her for *real* because he thinks girls getting detention is cool, which means I lost my date *and* my best friend and now it's clear to me Corey is going to continue humiliating me until I'm well into my nineties. How's your night going?"

Marty looked over at Cindy. "My date just popped a bubble and is peeling it off the top of her lip."

"Great. I'm happy for you. Enjoy your amazing life, Marty. If you'll excuse me, I'm going to go back to naming this wall."

"Trevor, stop. The answer is easy. Just tell Libby you'll fix this problem and go explain to the vice principal who switched the snacks."

Trevor looked up and spotted Corey now over by the

drink table, throwing back an entire bottle of orange soda.

"But that would be ratting out my own date, which can't be the classiest of maneuvers. And Libby thinks I'm a liar already, so she wouldn't ever believe that Molly did all of this. Corey would make sure of it."

Marty raised an eyebrow. "I told you before how to deal with a guy like Corey."

"No offense, Marty, but I tried to take your advice before and it didn't exactly work out."

"Not all of it. There is one part you seem to have forgotten." Marty knocked on Trevor's head, perhaps trying to rattle loose a memory. "The Jamie Jennison incident, when we were in the hall. Ring a bell?"

Trevor looked straight up to the ceiling hoping for a memory to break free from the ceiling tiles and fall down on him, ringing *something*.

Marty knew if Trevor stared at the ceiling long enough, the answer would come. It always worked for him. "Later, dude."

As Marty joined the rest of the crowd, Trevor stood by himself wondering how he could fix this. And wondering what piece of Marty's advice he'd forgotten. Because all Jamie did was ask him a question . . . he ignored her . . . she got upset . . .

Wait. The head knocking worked—his bell was rung!

Ignore him. Guys like Corey can't stand to be ignored.

"That's it! I'm supposed to ignore him!" Trevor said to himself, only he suddenly wasn't alone—Mr. Everett had walked up.

"Why is everyone wrapped up like Earth-toned mummies?" Mr. Everett was casually munching on some green Skittles.

"Someone switched the healthy snacks for Zingers and orange soda and now they're all amped up on sugar."

Mr. Everett shook his head. "Skittles are what they all need. It'll calm them right down. Too bad all my red ones are gone."

"No, Mr. Everett—" Trevor thought about explaining to him that Skittles do not create a calming effect on kids, but he was running out of time. He needed to get on with his plan of ignoring Corey so he could get Libby back on his side!

"Hope you find your red ones," Trevor said, then quickly walked up to the drink table and stood right next to Corey.

"Libby and I already have another date planned," Corey said. "Monday after her detention we're going to meet at the library . . . to do homework together." Corey did a little dance, like one of those end zone showboat dances that NFL players get heavily fined for. "Whatdaya think of that?"

As much as Trevor wanted to give Corey a lecture on the perils of being a jerk and how Libby would eventually see through his act and how one day in the distant future he would be defeated . . . he didn't. Instead he said nothing. *Nothing.* He didn't even give him a courtesy glance. Trevor simply ignored him . . . *completely* ignored him.

Trevor calmly picked up a bottle of orange soda and two cups and walked over to the bleachers. He figured Libby would be thirsty after all that salad dressing.

"Where are you going?" Corey called after him. "Get back here. I was talking to you, dude!"

Trevor gritted his teeth, trying to push through the temptation to turn around and respond to him. But Marty's advice floated above his head like a cloud puff of genius eighth grade wisdom. *Ignore him.*

Corey paced back and forth like a fenced-in stallion.

"I'm sorry, Libby." Trevor poured a cup of orange soda and held it out for her.

She looked up, her cheeks red. "I don't want anything to drink. I want to sit on these bleachers."

"You can't sit on the bleachers all night, Lib."

"I'm going to sit on these bleachers for eternity."

"Come on. Get up before you give the bleachers a name."

She tilted her head. "Why would I *name* them?"

Trevor blushed. "Uh. Never mind. Drink this." He shoved the drink in her hand. "Stay here. I'll fix everything."

"I already have a detention. What could be worse? There's no way I can get elected to student council with a blemish like this on my record. It's over."

It couldn't be. Trevor couldn't bear to watch Libby freak out over a detention she didn't deserve, give up on her goal of being elected student council president, and sit on bleachers that she might or might not soon give a name. "There *is* a way to fix it. Watch this."

Trevor spotted Molly across the room and ran over to her just before she pushed through the exit door. "Molly, wait!"

"This is lame. I'm going."

"I know you're my date and everything . . . and this is probably not the most romantic thing . . . but I'm going to have to tell the vice principal who did this." Trevor reached into her backpack, pulling out a handful of carrots. "Vice Principal Decker! Can you come here?"

"You're wasting your time." She shrugged, like she didn't really care. "He won't believe I did it. He never does."

Vice Principal Decker charged up to them. "What are these carrots doing in your hand, son?"

Trevor looked at Molly and gave her a sneaky smile. Even though he was shaking inside, he knew he had to do it. Molly may have been a severe rule-breaker, but like his mom said, girls have feelings—lots of them—and even though he didn't quite understand hers, he figured he could try. It was time for the guy to save the girl—both of them. "They're mine, sir. I was the one who switched the snacks. This is all my fault. I'm the one who should get detention, not Libby."

Mr. Everett, now snacking on Raspberry Zingers, joined them and interrupted. "Trevor? *You* did this?"

But Molly didn't let him answer. She couldn't help but think what Trevor had just done for her was the most interesting thing she'd ever seen. Or at least the most interesting thing that day. Either way, interesting was interesting, and she couldn't let Trevor take the blame for her. "Trevor didn't do it, Dad. *I* did it."

Vice Principal Decker put his hand on her shoulder. "Molly, that's enough. Do not take the blame for something someone else did. You're too nice of a girl sometimes." Pulling out a pink detention slip, Decker turned back to Trevor.

But Molly stepped up and tugged on her dad's elbow. "No, Dad. I did it. I did it all." She set her backpack down and unzipped it—out spilled Lefty, the enormous locker tool, Libby's Hola! Kitty Cat! sketchpad, Marty's *Extreme Hunter* magazine, troll dolls, snow globes, yo-yos, Koosh balls—practically the entire inventory of Toys "R" Us. Then she reached into her jean jacket pocket—she had a *lot* of pockets—and held her hand out to Mr. Everett, revealing its contents: forty-seven bite-size candies.

"My Skittles!" he yelped.

Molly then turned to face her dad. "I know you think I'm this perfect little girl. But this"—she motioned to the items spilled around on the floor—"*this* is who I am."

Decker placed his hand on her shoulder. "Every time we change schools you do something like this. You need to focus on making friends."

"I collect *things*, Dad—not friends." But Molly knew her dad wasn't listening—again. "Haven't you noticed all the stuff in my room that comes from nowhere? Do you notice *anything* about me?"

"I . . . I—"

Molly snatched a pink detention slip from his hand. "Thanks. I need this. Detention is the most interesting part of my day." She dropped the red Skittles into Mr. Everett's hand. "Sorry they're all sweaty. If you want to give me another detention—believe me—that would be fine."

Mr. Everett placed the Skittles into a Baggie he pulled

from his shirt pocket, apparently prepared for this special moment . . . the safe return of his dear red Skittles . . . and said, "No, Molly. I have a better way of keeping you from getting bored."

She folded her arms and shifted her weight to one leg—skeptic stance.

"Just as soon as you return all those thumbtacks you took from me, I'm going to have you decorate my bulletin board. It'll be your own personal art project. A way to *express* your boredom."

She shifted to the other leg, still not convinced.

He hesitated, then winced as he said, "And you'll have access to unlimited safety pins."

"Really?" She stuck her hand out. "Deal!" They shook—a sticky, gross, sweaty Skittle handshake deal.

Vice Principal Decker crossed his arms and paused for a moment as he studied Molly. Then he handed the rest of the detention slips to Mr. Everett. "Take over for me. And make sure the students get their belongings back." He led Molly to the door while students snuck over to the items scattered on the floor, and snatched their stolen stuff back like vultures. Decker looked down at her and said, "It sounds like we need to go home and have a talk." Then he shot her a wink. "And clean out that room of yours."

Molly pressed her lips together and held them there for a moment. Then looked up at her dad and said, "Some walking room would be nice."

Molly started to leave with him, but turned back and ran up to Trevor. "Thanks. No one's ever taken the blame for me. I thought no one would want to be friends with the new freaky bad kid. I guess I was wrong."

Trevor blushed. "Except I sort of ruined the night. I bet you wish you would've said yes to the other guy who asked you, huh?"

"Corey? No way. I don't go to dances with jerks," she said as she punched him lightly on the shoulder and ran off.

Wait. Trevor shuddered. *COREY was the one who asked Molly?*

Trevor Jones

At the drink table,
pacing as he drinks
an orange soda

8:01 p.m.

That's why Corey has been torturing me—he was
jealous that Molly wanted to go to the dance with
ME. He liked her. And now that he likes Libby,
he'll do whatever it takes to keep her away from
me too.

No. No way. Libby and I have spent every holiday
together—including Presidents' Day—since we were
born. He can't stop a friendship like that.

CHAPTER TWENTY-FIVE

TREVOR TURNED AROUND AND SAW **C**OREY SAUNTERING over to Libby again.

Oh, no.

Trevor ran toward them, hoping to get to her in time, but Corey got there first. Libby was now standing, rocking from foot to foot, clearly amped up on sugar from her orange soda. He could hear Libby as she said to Corey, "Did you hear? Cindy just told me that Trevor got Molly to admit she did it! I don't have detention now!"

Corey took a step back. "Wait, now you *don't* have detention?"

"No! Isn't that great?! And Trevor even found the carrots. We can put the Zingers away!"

Trevor joined up with them, a little out of breath, and

smiled at Libby. "That's right. You can rip up that detention slip, Lib."

She smiled back at him. A big, happy, amped-up-on-orange soda smile.

Corey waved them off. "Naw, this is stupid. I'm not eating any carrots and I'm not going out with some girl who *doesn't* get detention. I can get algebra answers from someone cooler."

Libby planted her hands on her hips. "What are you *talking* about?"

He stepped back. "Nothing. Forget it."

But she took a step closer and narrowed her eyes. "Tell me. Now."

He huffed. "Look, I only took you to this dumb dance so you'd give me algebra answers, but then I thought you were cool for doing all this and getting detention, but I was wrong." He shook his head. "You're *not* cool, Libby."

Libby turned away from him and Trevor could see her eyes were filling with tears. He had only seen Libby cry one other time. And that was when he ran over her toes in third grade when he was trying to impress her with his No Hands bike skills, skills he didn't actually have. So she yelped and cried in pain when he smooshed her, which Trevor felt was understandable and never told anyone.

But Trevor knew these tears Corey had caused weren't going to be stopped with an ice pack and his half of the cherry Fun Dip. He decided he wasn't going to ever let Corey Long make Libby cry again.

Immediately Trevor thought about punching his lights out—an obvious choice—but he knew there was only one thing that would actually hurt Corey Long: embarrassment.

But when Trevor looked up, he saw his mom, busy unwrapping students from streamers and trying to convince them to limit their orange soda intake to *just one*. And as she looked up, she caught his eye, giving him a thumbs-up. A gesture that seared right into his chest, because he knew what he was about to do would get him in trouble, and disappointing his mom would cause the glaciers to melt.

But there were times to break the rules—even right in front of your own mother—if it was for the right reason. Because at that moment, he decided the whole "getting through middle school" thing didn't come down to perfectly scuffed shoes or who he asked to the dance or if he didn't doodle or talk about baseball cards.

It came down to being epic at the right moment.

Trevor picked up the bottle of orange soda, took a step closer, held the bottle high, and poured it directly over Corey's head, drenching every single one of his perfectly placed hairs. "That's where you're wrong: she *is* cool," Trevor said.

Wow, Trevor thought. The right words finally came out!

Just then Mr. Everett charged up to them. "Trevor, you can't—"

"It's okay." Trevor held his hand out. "I don't mind getting detention for this."

Corey screamed, "My hair!" He clenched his wet locks of hair in his hands, then ran off through the crowd and into the bathroom. But with his hair in his eyes—in the bad way, not the good way—and unable to see, he made an unfortunate wrong turn.

The shrieking was rather ear-piercing.

Libby laughed, *really* laughed, then sat back down on the bleachers and kept on laughing. Trevor wished he could've recorded it; it was one of those laughs he would want to replay for her over and over years from now when they were hanging out in the nursing home. Playing video games.

Trevor stepped up to Mr. Everett, and the teacher placed the elusive pink slip in his hand, but before Trevor could even put it in his pocket, his mom barreled up to him. "Trevor!"

"Mom, I can explain—"

She held her hand up. "You don't have to. Part of Decker's chaperone training included lip reading—to detect bad language. I know why you got that detention."

Trevor squinted at her, not sure where she was going with this.

She winked. "It's okay. Sometimes I break the rules for the right reasons too."

He was relieved this wasn't sending her into a disappointment spiral. "Thanks, Mom."

She put her hands on her hips and surveyed the room. "But it was your date who did this."

"How'd you know?"

"Molly told me—ran over to me on her way out. She said she guessed something big was about to happen between you and Corey . . . something about her seeing these types of things before. So she wanted to make sure I knew *why* you did what you were about to do." Ms. Jones took a deep breath, a little exhausted by the whole explanation. And also a little confused. "So your date . . . she's athletic *and psychic?*"

He let out a big sigh, relieved that Molly—who acted like she didn't want to be a friend—had done just that. "She's not psychic. She's just been to *a lot* of schools."

Ms. Jones folded her arms contentedly. "Well, she's not what I expected, but if she's *anything,* at least she's *interesting.*"

Exactly, Trevor thought.

Ms. Jones patted him on the back then moved back into the crowd, unwrapping students trapped in their streamers.

When she was gone, Libby strolled up next to him and punched him on the arm.

"Ouch!" *Do* all *girls think guys like being hit?*

"That's for not telling me earlier Corey Long was a jerk!"

He rubbed his arm. "I did . . . twice!"

"And *this—*"

Trevor flinched, preparing for a face slap or foot stomp.

"This . . . is for being a good friend." She smiled and handed him a Raspberry Zinger. It was smooshed, but it was edible.

He opened it and smirked at her. "I'm a friend, huh?"

She briefly closed her eyes and took a quick breath, then blurted, "I shouldn't have told you we weren't *friend* friends anymore. I figured it would be a good thing. But I was wrong."

"You do realize I had no idea what it meant?"

She laughed. "I didn't either."

Trevor calmly took a bite of the Raspberry Zinger, feeling relieved. "So I'm back to being your friend?"

She lightly punched him one more time on the arm. "The best."

His arm was starting to go numb from all the light punching, but he was glad to get punched at all. Maybe deep, deep down, guys really *do* like it when girls hit them. *Maybe.* "Thanks, Lib."

He considered breaking the news to her that he knew she hadn't thrown away her Hola! Kitty Cat! sketchpad because it was still sitting on the gym floor where Molly had left it—but spilling that secret might result in full-effort punching and his arm really did hurt, so instead he reached into his pocket. "Carrot?"

She smiled and pulled out a cup of ranch dressing. And the two sat on the bleachers, eating snacks, and watching the chaos.

"Trevor?"

"Yeah?"

"I figured it out."

"What's that?"

"Bleacher-y. We shall call him Bleacher-y, and he is our friend."

He nodded. "It's a good name, Libby . . . a very good name."

Corey Long

In the hallway,
drying his hair
with a paper towel

8:08 p.m.

Okay, so maybe I deserved that, but did he have to
go for the HAIR? Is he trying to RUIN me?!

So yeah, I get it . . . he thinks I'm the evil
one.

I'm Darth Vader.

But that's okay. Because really, if you think
about it . . . Vader's the coolest.

True, he dies by getting burned by a shaft of
lightning.

But come on . . . dude is COOL. Hey, some of us
are just born that way.

Cindy Applegate

Party cleanup
duty, seemingly
enjoying it

8:10 p.m.

Okay, okay, so I heard he poured a five-gallon bottle of orange soda over Corey's head and then unwrapped like three Zingers and smashed them in his face. Which is gross because I heard one of them was the coconut flavor and that is just . . . ewww. Coconut?! It does horrible things for your complexion. Even if I were trapped on a desert island with only palm trees and coconuts, I would never put them in a Zinger and eat them. Much less let them get near my face.

Then I also heard Trevor tripped Corey so hard that Corey did one of those 300-degree somersaults in the air, and the fall caused his hair to look totally out of place for, like, a whole minute. Then Trevor locked him in the janitor's Supply Containment Unit. That's what I heard.

[scratches her head nervously, blinks repetitively]

Okay, fine, yes, I MADE UP some of that. I do that sometimes, but it's not like anyone actually listens to me. I'm too short. That's why I want to win student council president. It's the only way people will pay attention to me.

Wanna know my slogan? Here goes . . . Gum makes you smart. Legalize gum.

I know . . . there's NO WAY I can lose. For reals.

Baker Twins

7th graders
Waiting for their
mom to pick them up

8:15 p.m.

Brian: Naw, dude. I heard Trevor went all ninja on him and pulled out the nunchucks.

Brad: No, no. It was a couple of ballpoint pens.

Brian: They were nunchucks, dude.

Brad: No, I heard it loud and clear. Trevor pulled out two blue ballpoint pens and chased him down the street.

Brian: Pens? That doesn't even make sense!

Brad: Wait. Never mind. I was thinking about something I saw on TV. You're right. It was nunchucks.

Brian: No, dude. I was kidding. Totally made that up.

Brad: Funny. You clearly inherited the funny genes.

Brian: And you inherited the Way Too Uptight genes, bro.

Brad: You're wearing my shoes.

Brian: I want my shirt back.

Trevor Jones

Cleaning up orange
streamers, looking
around for extra
Raspberry Zingers

8:17 p.m.

No, I didn't pull out ballpoint pens or trip him
or smash his face with Zingers. Yes, I poured some
orange soda over him. Yes, he ran off. Yes, into
the girls' bathroom. But that was it.

Except I did hear about the nunchucks rumor.
And, uh . . . I think I'm gonna let that one stick
around for a bit longer.

A little nunchucks rumor couldn't hurt anyone's reputation.

Certainly not mine.

Wait. I have a reputation??!!

[fist-pump]

YESSSSS!!!

CHAPTER TWENTY-SIX

O N MONDAY AFTERNOON TREVOR WALKED INTO detention after school. And standing next to the door waiting for him was Libby.

"What are you doing here? You missed the bus!" he said.

"I'll wait out here for you. I figured you might want some company on the way home." Libby leaned in and added, "And you know how I told you to make a new friend?"

He shifted his backpack nervously. "Uh, yeah . . . see the thing about that—"

"I don't know if you realize it, but I think you did."

"Huh?"

She had a sneaky grin on her face as she sauntered off down the hall to get a drink of water. Trevor didn't know what she meant until he had sat down in his chair. Glancing at the door, Trevor saw Marty standing there, feet planted shoulder-width apart, with a note held high.

As always, Libby was right.

Miss Plimp suddenly dropped her chalk. "Marty!"

Oh, no. He was caught. That was a detention for sure.

"Close that door. There's a draft!!"

Libby and Trevor

Waiting at the
bus stop

7:52 a.m.

(Quite talkative
for so early in
the morning)

Libby: So Trevor was the one trying to loosen up.
But really, that's what I needed to do. I was
the one who needed to change—not him.

Trevor: You do realize the camera is running.
They're recording this. You can't take it back.

Libby: I'm not going to be so color-coordinated
anymore. Maybe extreme overplanning isn't the
way to go.

Trevor: Does that mean you're not going to be in
charge of my life anymore?

Libby: Oh, I'll still be your social director.
That's a permanent position. In fact, do you
still have your lucky Uni-ball pen?

Trevor: I know, I know . . . no more drawing.

Libby: Actually, I think you should keep using it.
I like your drawings.

Trevor: Fine, I'll throw it away . . . wait. What?

Libby: It's cool. You're good at doodling.
Trevor.

[Trevor races off.]

Libby: Trevor? Trevor! TREVOR! Get back here! I
didn't mean go do it NOW!!

The artichoke loaf was spotted
in the front seat of the lunch
lady's car wearing a hat and
fake mustache. We believe
she is using leftovers as a
cover to use the carpool lane.

ROBIN MELLOM used to teach middle schoolers and now she writes about them. (Any resemblance between fictional characters and her previous real-life students is purely coincidental. Probably.) She is also the author of *Ditched: A Love Story*. She lives with her husband and son on the Central Coast of California. Learn more at www.robinmellom.com and follow her on Twitter (@robinmellom).

Through a freak incident involving a school bus, a Labrador retriever, and twenty-four rolls of toilet paper, **STEPHEN GILPIN** knew that someday he would be an artist. He applied himself diligently and many years later, he has found himself the illustrator of around thirty children's books. He lives in Hiawatha, Kansas, with his genius wife, Angie, and a whole bunch of kids. Visit his Web site at www.sgilpin.com.